THE ULTIMATE GUIDE

WARRIORS

EXPLORE THE

WARRIORS

WORLD

WARRIORS

THE ULTIMATE GUIDE

ERIN HUNTER
ILLUSTRATED BY WAYNE McLOUGHLIN

HARPER
An Imprint of HarperCollinsPublishers

Special thanks to Victoria Holmes

The Ultimate Guide
Text copyright © 2013 by Working Partners Limited
Illustrations copyright © 2013 by Wayne McLoughlin
Series created by Working Partners Limited

www.harpercollinschildrens.com
ISBN 978-0-06-224533-5 (trade bdg.)
Typography by Megan Stitt
16 17   SCP   10 9 8 7 6 5
❖
First Edition

CONTENTS

✦

SHADOWCLAN

WINDCLAN

RIVERCLAN

SKYCLAN

TRIBE OF RUSHING WATER

THE EARLY SETTLERS

ANIMALS OUTSIDE THE CLANS

HIGHSTONES

BARLEY'S FARM

WINDCLAN CAMP

FOURTREES

FALLS

OWL-TREE

RIVER

SUNNING-ROCKS

RIVERCLAN CAMP

THE FOREST

CARRIONPLACE

SHADOWCLAN
CAMP

THUNDERPATH

THUNDERCLAN
CAMP

GREAT
SYCAMORE

SANDY
HOLLOW

SNAKEROCKS

TALLPINES

TREECUT PLACE

TWOLEGPLACE

THUNDERCLAN

RIVERCLAN

SHADOWCLAN

WINDCLAN

STARCLAN

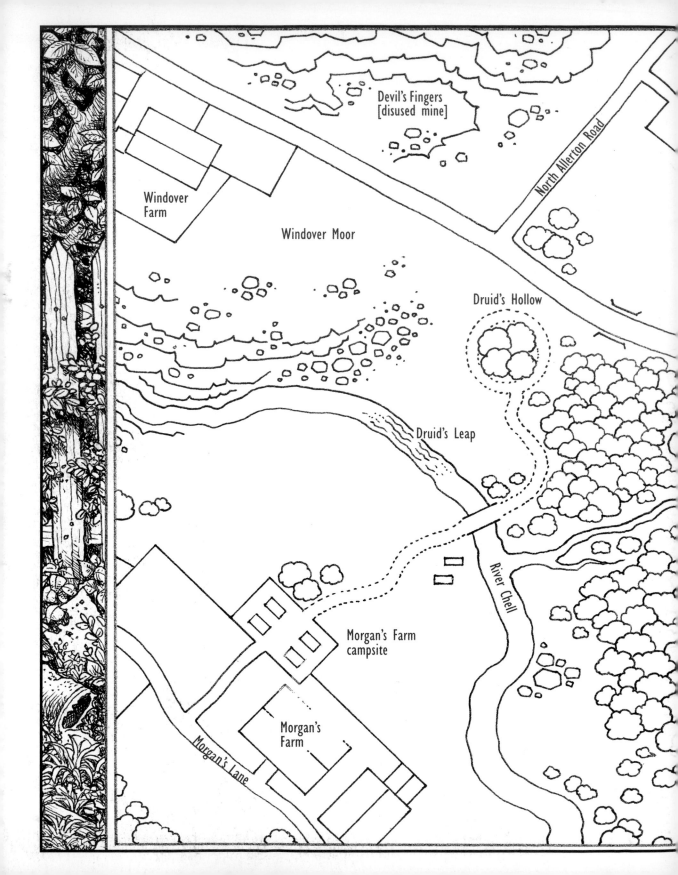

Devil's Fingers
[disused mine]

North Allerton Road

Windover Farm

Windover Moor

Druid's Hollow

Druid's Leap

River Chell

Morgan's Farm campsite

Morgan's Lane

Morgan's Farm

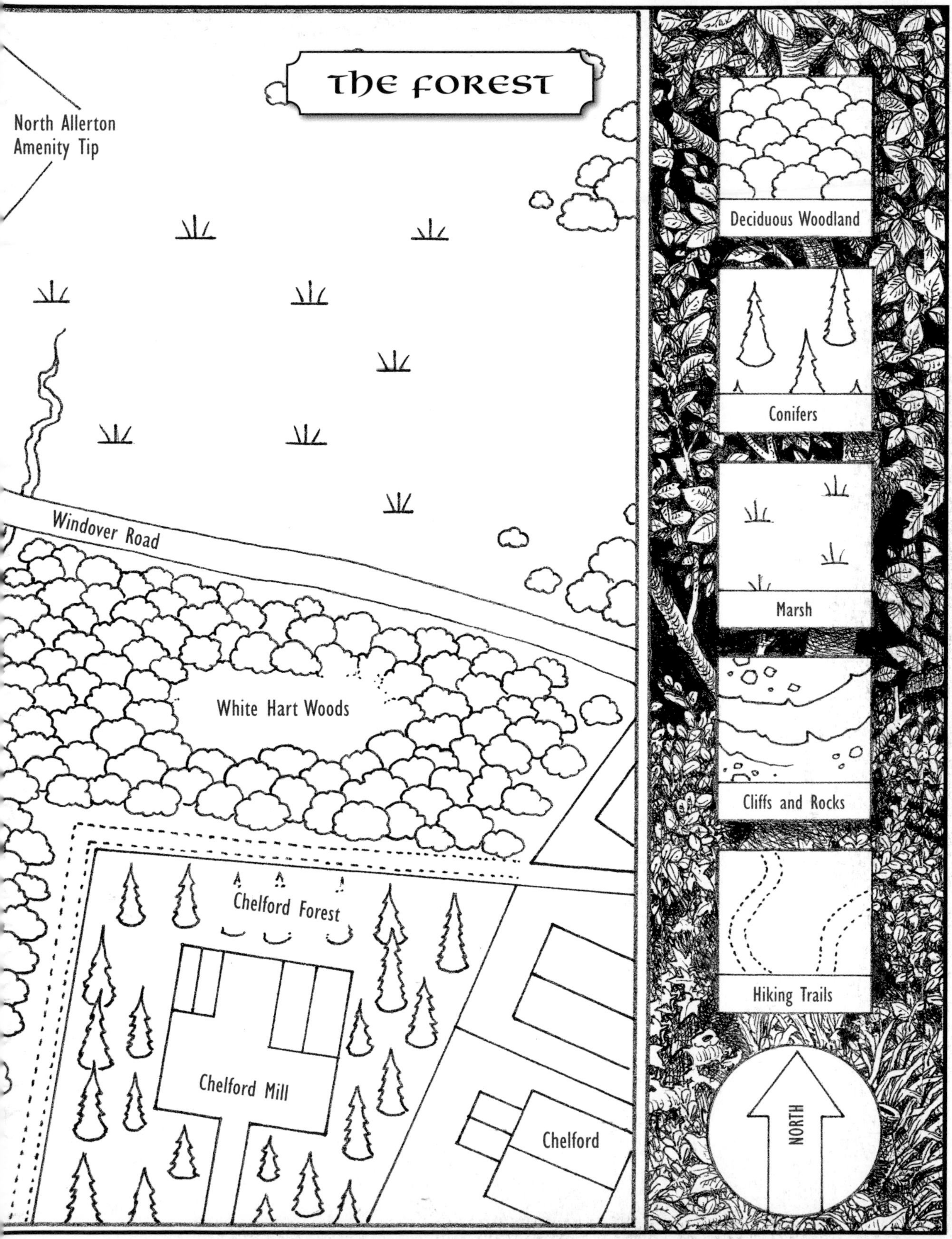

THE FOREST

North Allerton
Amenity Tip

Windover Road

White Hart Woods

Chelford Forest

Chelford Mill

Chelford

Legend

Deciduous Woodland

Conifers

Marsh

Cliffs and Rocks

Hiking Trails

NORTH

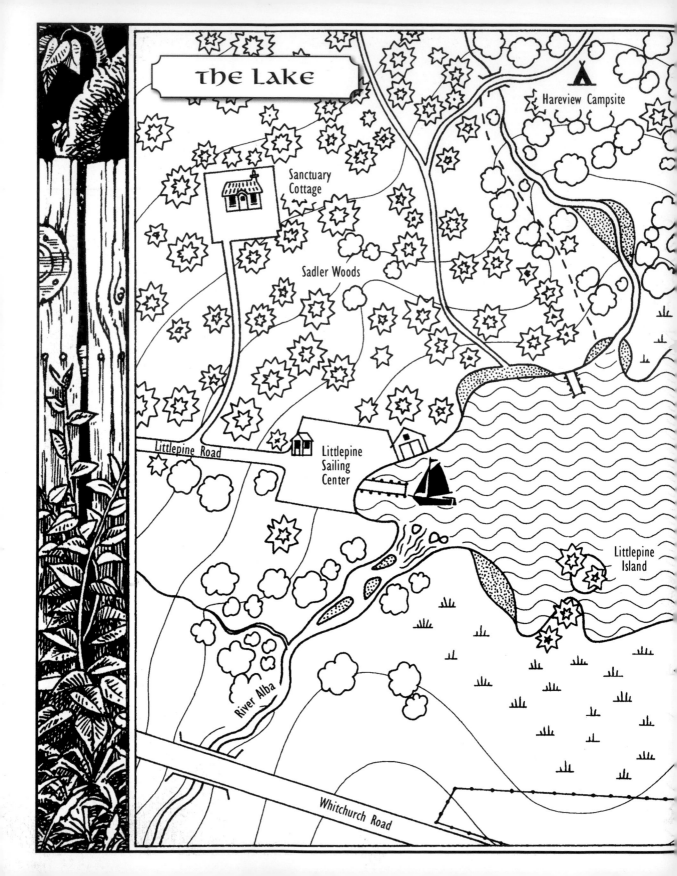

The Lake

Hareview Campsite

Sanctuary Cottage

Sadler Woods

Littlepine Road

Littlepine Sailing Center

Littlepine Island

River Alba

Whitchurch Road

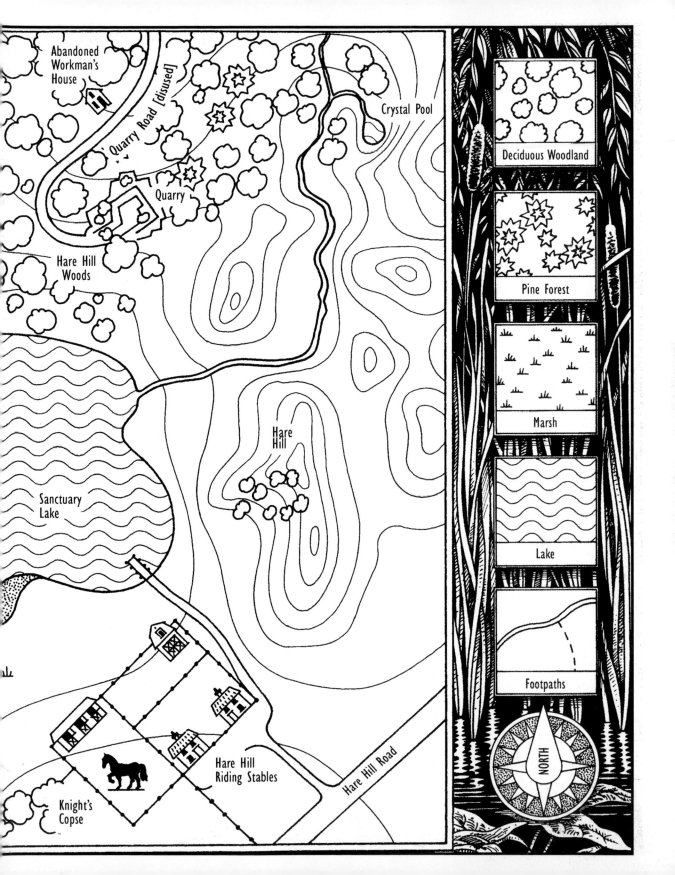

Abandoned
Workman's
House

Quarry Road [disused]

Crystal Pool

Quarry

Hare Hill
Woods

Hare
Hill

Sanctuary
Lake

Hare Hill
Riding Stables

Hare Hill Road

Knight's
Copse

Deciduous Woodland

Pine Forest

Marsh

Lake

Footpaths

NORTH

SKYROCK

LEADER'S DEN

SKY'S DEN

THE GORGE

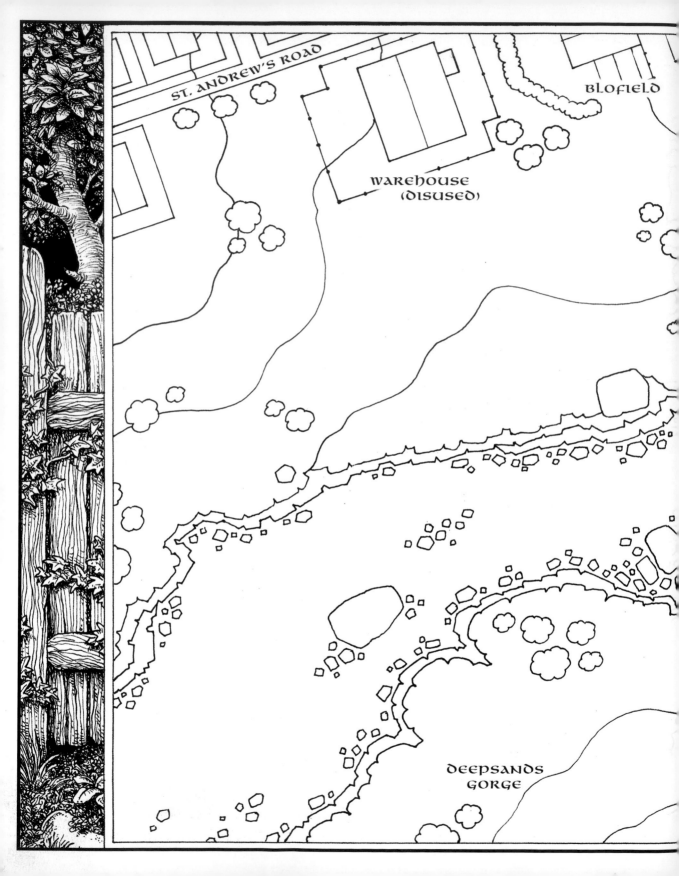

ST. ANDREW'S ROAD

BLOFIELD

WAREHOUSE
(DISUSED)

DEEPSANDS
GORGE

SOUTH BLOFIELD ROAD

BLOFIELD HEATH

HIGH DENE WOODS

WARNING: UNSTABLE CLIFFS IN THIS AREA

RIVER CHEL

DEEPSANDS POOL

THE GORGE

INTRODUCTION

THERE WERE FOUR CLANS that lived in a forest. Each Clan defended a territory that best suited its hunting skills: Fleet-footed rabbit chasers lived on the moor below broad open skies; glossy-furred cats who were happy to get their paws wet in search of fish settled beside the river; stalkers of mice and squirrels made their home among dense trees and tangled undergrowth; and bold, cunning cats who had a taste for frogs patrolled the marshes fringed by brittle pine trees.

But no . . . there were originally *five* Clans. One Clan was forced out when Twolegs took over its territory. That Clan, the tree-hunters, created a new home far, far away in a sandy gorge.

And before those five Clans, there was a community of cats living deep in the mountains, beneath an endlessly tumbling waterfall. These cats had left their home beside a lake after a hard-won decision to find somewhere else to live, free from black-and-white dogs that were too easily diverted from chasing sheep into chasing cats instead.

Those four Clans that lived in the forest? They ended up beside the very same lake when Twolegs rampaged through their territories, flattening trees to make space for a new Thunderpath. With their distant ancestors lost from memory, the Clans believed they were the first cats to settle there, forging new paths among the trees and across the windy hills.

Everywhere the cats have been, there are layers upon layers of history—some known, some long-forgotten, and some discovered in the most unexpected ways—laid down by the paw steps of many generations. What shaped the lives of these proud and noble warriors? Come, walk among them for a while, and listen to their stories. . . .

THUNDERCLAN

Introduction to ThunderClan: Bluestar Speaks

LIKE ALL OF THE Clans, ThunderClan has been shaped by the nature of its home, by the dense forest and prey-rich thickets that lie between its boundaries. My warriors are the most skilled predators of any Clan, able to make themselves silent and invisible in order to hunt the tiny furred and feathered creatures that live among us. They can stalk over fallen leaves and brittle twigs without making a sound, and from a standstill they can pounce with enough strength to bring down a full-grown rabbit. We are descended from the cats who were most adept at hunting beneath the trees, who were undaunted by branches blocking out the sky and the need to fight enemies at close quarters when there was no open space in which to escape an attacker. This battling in close quarters gave us courage and confidence in our abilities to feed and defend ourselves, and we knew the forest was the right home for us.

It was the warrior code that let us grow as a Clan and maintain our beloved forest territory. No Clan guards the code as passionately as ThunderClan. To our dying breath, we know it will protect us from injustice, cruelty, and needless battles. The code tells us to check our boundaries daily, and prohibits trespassing or hunting on another Clan's territory, and we follow this. The other Clans might call us cowards for avoiding constant border skirmishes, but we would fight for our territory as fiercely as any of them—just not when a more peaceful answer can be found by obeying the code that we share.

When we lived in the forest beside Twolegplace, our greatest border quarrel was with RiverClan over Sunningrocks. When cats first came to the forest, these rocks were an island in the middle of the river, accessible only to those peculiar cats who were willing to swim to it. But the river changed its course, and the rocks were soon attached by dry land to ThunderClan territory. The only logical conclusion was that they should be absorbed into our borders. RiverClan, those fish-eating mouse-brains, insisted this was unfair and tried bitterly to reclaim Sunningrocks. We won more of those battles than we lost, which speaks for itself. When my warriors know they are in the right, they will fight like lions.

But we also know what it is like to be without the boundaries of a Clan. Living so close to Twolegplace in the forest, we met more kittypets than the other Clans, and had more rogues passing through. I tried to teach my Clan to treat these strangers as cats just like us before judging them for where they were born. Compared to some of the dark-hearted warriors clawing at our borders, there are better cats who have no belief in StarClan at all. Cats can learn to follow the warrior code, but they cannot always learn to have the compassion or courage that comes from faith.

BLUESTAR

BLUESTAR

LEADER OF THUNDERCLAN BEFORE Firestar, Bluestar was a proud and deeply committed warrior. Once known as Bluefur, her early life was scarred by tragedy. Her mother was killed during a raid on WindClan and soon after, her sister, Snowfur, died on the Thunderpath. Isolated in her grief from her own Clanmates, Bluefur fell in love with a RiverClan warrior named Oakheart, but their brief relationship ended when Bluefur realized she could not be loyal to ThunderClan while her heart lay elsewhere. Unbeknownst to Bluefur, she was already expecting Oakheart's kits.

Bluefur paid the highest possible price for her leadership, giving up her three tiny kits in order to become deputy instead of Thistleclaw, whom she feared would destroy ThunderClan with his dark-hearted ambition. Oakheart raised Stonefur and Mistyfoot, the two kits who survived, in his own Clan. Bluefur told her Clanmates that her litter had been stolen by a starving badger, and then overcame her sadness to become deputy and leader as she had hoped.

When Bluestar was an apprentice, the ThunderClan medicine cat Goosefeather had delivered a prophecy to her: "You will blaze through the forest like fire; only water can destroy you." During her leadership, as ThunderClan struggled against its rivals, Bluestar looked to another source of fire—the red-pelted kittypet Rusty—to save her beloved Clan. But Bluestar's murderous deputy Tigerclaw continued to rage against ThunderClan even after becoming leader of ShadowClan. He set a pack of ravenous dogs to raid the camp, and Bluestar gave up her ninth life to lead the dogs over the edge of the gorge, dying for the last time in water, just as Goosefeather had foretold. StarClan showed enough mercy that Stonefur and Mistyfoot found Bluestar on RiverClan's shore, and her final moments were spent making peace with her surviving children before she went to join her lost daughter, Mosskit, in StarClan.

← # Bluestar Takes Selfies

PINESTAR

PINESTAR

PINESTAR WAS THE LEADER of ThunderClan when Bluekit (later Bluestar) was born. He was fiercely protective of ThunderClan's borders and prey, but preferred a show of strength via patrols and words rather than actual conflict to resolve any issues. Pinestar was a calm, fair-minded leader, resigned to doing battle with RiverClan over Sunningrocks, and confident in the abilities of his deputy, Sunfall, to organize the Clan's daily routine. When his medicine cat Goosefeather found a sign that warned WindClan was on the verge of destroying ThunderClan, Pinestar reluctantly agreed to take action. Several of his senior warriors were eager to invade WindClan and teach them exactly what would come of stealing prey from ThunderClan, but Pinestar knew how much this would cost his Clanmates in injuries and even death.

Pinestar led the attack on WindClan himself, and the battle turned out to be as bloody as he had feared, with the death of Bluepaw's mother, Moonflower, at the claws of WindClan's warrior-turned-medicine cat, Hawkheart. The battle was lost, and Pinestar grew increasingly disillusioned with the violence and contrasting fragility of Clan life. He started roaming beyond the borders of ThunderClan, crossing into Twolegplace and observing the easy lives of the kittypets who didn't have to risk their lives for the sake of food and shelter.

Pinestar was befriended by a kittypet named Jake, who was intrigued by the cats in the woods and had once traveled for a while with Talltail, a warrior from WindClan. Pinestar started to take food from a Twoleg, and gradually life outside the Clan became more and more appealing. His travels couldn't stay secret for long, though, and he was spotted on one of his Twolegplace visits by a young ThunderClan apprentice named

← KITTYPETS!

Lionpaw. Embarrassed, Pinestar lied that he was engaged in a long battle with a kitty-pet, and was just pretending to be one himself in order to pass unchallenged through Twolegplace.

But yet another invasion of Sunningrocks by RiverClan made Pinestar realize that he could not spend his last life fighting for every paw step of territory and every mouthful of food. His greatest regret was leaving behind his kits with Leopardfoot, especially the little tom, Tigerkit, who was already fierce and bold and eager to fight. Pinestar handed over leadership of his Clan to Sunfall, then left to live with his adopted Twoleg. Pinestar believed he had served his Clan loyally and well for eight long lives, and he deserved some peace at the end.

GOOSEFEATHER and
FEATHERWHISKER

← Goose whisher
and Feather feather# GOOSEFEATHER AND FEATHERWHISKER

GOOSEFEATHER AND HIS APPRENTICE, Featherwhisker, were medicine cats during Pinestar's leadership of ThunderClan. Goosefeather was a naturally skilled medicine cat, but by old age he became better known for his laziness and sour temper than for his original talents. He took a close interest in Bluefur, who would one day become Bluestar, and her sister, Snowfur, because their mother, Moonflower, was his littermate.

Goosefeather had a habit of interpreting omens in the darkest way, and in the end, it was his doom-laden prophecy that led to the battle with WindClan, and Moonflower's death. Goosefeather interpreted the flattened fur on a vole from the fresh-kill pile as a sign that WindClan would crush ThunderClan, kill all the warriors and destroy their territory. Strong feelings stirred up in the Clan left Pinestar with no option but to attack WindClan first. A second omen—a shred of catmint on the vole's flank—was seen by Goosefeather as a warning from StarClan that they must invade the very heart of WindClan, inside their camp, and destroy their supply of herbs. It was a bold plan and ultimately disastrous, leading to death and defeat for the ThunderClan warriors. Goosefeather was unrepentant, insisting that his omens were correct.

Soon after the battle with WindClan, a branch was struck by lightning and fell, burning, between Bluepaw and a threatening fox. Rain swiftly came to extinguish the fire, and Bluepaw and the woods were saved. To Goosefeather, this was a prophecy about Bluepaw herself: that she would blaze through the forest like fire, quenched only by water. Bluepaw had no inclination to take his words seriously, not after he had prompted the battle that killed her mother.

From that moment on, Goosefeather's mind wandered from the dedication and curiosity essential for a medicine cat, and his Clan turned more and more to his apprentice, Featherwhisker, instead. Goosefeather retreated into a world of sinister omens, and an unfailing conviction that ThunderClan was on the brink of destruction. Featherwhisker took over all medicine duties with a calmness and sense of optimism that had been missing in his mentor. Goosefeather's final act of madness was to react with horror whenever he was in the presence of Tigerkit, Pinestar and Leopardfoot's sole remaining son. He confided to Bluefur that Tigerkit should never have been born, and he urged Bluefur to become deputy instead of the ambitious warrior Thistleclaw, whatever it took.

Whether he interpreted omens correctly or not, Goosefeather shaped the future of ThunderClan by setting Bluefur on the course of her destiny. But she was glad to have Featherwhisker by her side by the time she received her nine lives as leader of her Clan.

FIRESTAR

FIRESTAR

THIS BRAVE, BIGHEARTED THUNDERCLAN leader started life as a kittypet named Rusty, and lived with housefolk for his first six moons. He inherited his father Jake's fascination with what lay beyond the Twoleg nests, in the woods where wild cats were rumored to live. A chance encounter with a ThunderClan apprentice named Graypaw led to an introduction to Bluestar, who saw in the young kittypet's flame-colored pelt echoes of a recent prophecy: "Fire alone will save the Clan."

Renamed Firepaw, and then Fireheart, the young ginger cat trained hard to become one of ThunderClan's most trusted warriors, and later, Bluestar's deputy. But his path was darkened by a feud with Tigerclaw, the former deputy who was driven out of the Clan when Fireheart uncovered his plot to kill Bluestar.

Firepaw's closest friends in the moons following his arrival were Graypaw, Ravenpaw, and the young medicine cat, Spottedleaf. After Spottedleaf's death during a ShadowClan raid, he grew close to a feisty, russet-furred she-cat named Sandstorm, and soon after Fireheart became leader and took on the name Firestar, she gave birth to his daughters, Leafkit and Squirrelkit.

Firestar led ThunderClan during the Great Journey from the forest to the lake and helped to establish all four Clans in their new homes. His untiring faith in StarClan gave him strength to fight against illnesses, drought, Twoleg disturbances, and border clashes. Except for one life lost to illness, he gave each of his nine lives for the sake of his Clanmates—most of all his final life, lost in the battle against the Dark Forest. A blaze of lightning marked the moment that Firestar joined his warrior ancestors—ancestors not by blood, but by heritage, honor, and tradition.

SPOTTEDLEAF

SPOTTEDLEAF

SPOTTEDLEAF WAS THE MEDICINE cat in ThunderClan when Rusty the kitty-pet, who would one day become Firestar, first arrived. She saw in him the same qualities that Bluestar did: courage, spirit, unwavering loyalty to doing the right thing. But Spottedleaf also saw Rusty as a warm, sensitive cat who was not limited by his expectations of her role as medicine cat and who viewed her more than anything else as a friend. If things had been different—if Spottedleaf had been a few moons younger, an apprentice warrior rather than a medicine cat—their relationship would have become even closer.

Instead, Spottedleaf died before she and Fireheart could find a way to express how they felt about each other, which left her frustrated and lonely in StarClan, missing the friend she had left behind. She refused to let go of the connection she had shared with Fireheart, and walked in his dreams, guiding and supporting him in his early days of leading ThunderClan.

When Firestar left to rediscover SkyClan, Spottedleaf knew she had lost him to Sandstorm. In her heart, she understood that the young she-cat was a far better choice, able to walk side by side with Firestar, bear his kits, and share responsibility for the Clan over the coming seasons. Spottedleaf grieved for missed chances, for a life that could never have been, but she still watched over Firestar and her former Clanmates as they moved to the lake and built new lives far from her forest home.

In the final confrontation with the Dark Forest, Spottedleaf gave her life in the stars to save Sandstorm, one last gift to her beloved Firestar.

← Stalker

GRAYSTRIPE AND
MILLIE

GRAYSTRIPE AND MILLIE

AS AN APPRENTICE, GRAYPAW'S boldness and bravery led him to be the first Clan cat to approach Rusty the kittypet, who went on to become Firestar. This boldness would lead him into trouble more than once—but it was the same courage and impulsive generosity that moved him and Fireheart to catch food for RiverClan when the river was poisoned, and to travel far beyond the territories to rescue WindClan after they had been chased out by ShadowClan.

Like Bluestar, Graystripe fell in love with a RiverClan cat: Silverstream, daughter of Crookedstar. Silverstream died giving birth to Graystripe's kits, Stormkit and Featherkit, and when ThunderClan failed to treat these kits with the kindness that Graystripe hoped for, he took them back to their mother's Clan. It tore him apart to leave his Clan—and his best friend, Fireheart—but he believed that RiverClan was the only place where they'd be truly welcomed. Stormkit and Featherkit thrived, eventually taking the warrior names Stormfur and Feathertail, but Graystripe returned to ThunderClan when he realized that his loyalties were not to his kits' Clan, but to his own.

When Twolegs began to destroy the forest to make way for a new Thunderpath, they set traps for the cats in their way. Graystripe was captured while risking his life to free others, and was taken away to live with Twolegs. Although treated kindly, he never forgot that he was a warrior and always yearned to find the Clan he had lost.

While imprisoned by Twolegs, he met a kittypet named Millie who loved him enough to travel with him all the way to the lake where the Clans had made new homes. Graystripe was welcomed like a returning hero, but it was Millie's determination that got them out of Twolegplace, and her untiring encouragement that helped Graystripe find his lost Clanmates. Millie quickly learned to hunt for prey and fight as well as any warrior, but she refused to take a warrior name or be ashamed of where she had come from. Because of this, some cats always questioned her loyalty to the warrior code—though never within earshot of Graystripe.

↤ Worst mother

SANDSTORM

← bossy ar

SANDSTORM

WHEN RUSTY THE KITTYPET first joined ThunderClan, Sandpaw sided with fellow apprentice Dustpaw in tormenting him. But the former kittypet, who would eventually come to be known as Firestar, soon made a very different impression on her, as she began to appreciate his courage and loyalty to his adopted Clan. He slowly came to realize how important she was to him as well, and Sandstorm's friendship and support were especially important to Firestar as he prepared for the battle against BloodClan. Firestar was determined to save the forest from Scourge and had heard StarClan's prophecy that he was the only one who could do so. But Sandstorm was the cat who made Firestar believe that he was doing the right thing by fighting the cats from Twolegplace and that he would be able to defeat them.

Sandstorm was a proud and committed warrior and her courage equaled Firestar's on the journey to rebuild SkyClan in the sandy gorge far from the forest. Sandstorm took on the role of medicine cat to help the scattered Clanmates, and she matched Firestar blow for blow in the battle against the rats, even though she had only a single life to lose. She was an excellent mother to Squirrelflight and Leafpool, and stood by her daughters when the truth came out about Lionblaze, Hollyleaf, and Jayfeather.

Sandstorm had a quick temper and a strong sense of what was right, which Firestar respected. Next to his deputies and his medicine cats, Sandstorm was the cat he consulted most often before making any decisions for the Clan. She spoke up for the cats in ThunderClan who shied away from the traditional warrior lifestyle, in particular Daisy, who came from the horseplace by the lake. Sandstorm defended Daisy's wish to stay in the nursery and help other queens, instead of joining border or hunting patrols.

Sandstorm would have loved to have had more kits, but she knew that Firestar had enough demands made on him by the rest of the Clan. She shared his sense of responsibility to all of the cats who lived in the hollow, and never wished that their lives could have been different.

BRIGHTHEART

BRIGHTHEART AND CLOUDTAIL

BRIGHTHEART'S RAVAGED FACE REMINDED every cat of the attack from Tigerstar's half-trained pack of dogs. But Brightheart only remembered when she saw her reflection in a pool of water—so she avoided drinking from anything except fast-flowing streams. She tried hard to forget the horror and pain of the mauling, and to ignore the flinches that came from strangers seeing her for the first time. Far from being treated like an invalid, Brightheart hunted and fought alongside her Clanmates and spent time with every apprentice, training them in specialized battle skills to use if one of their own eyes were injured. She possessed the true beauty that comes from courage, loyalty, and devotion—but she had no wish to see her own face.

Happily, despite her scars, Brightheart's life turned into everything she ever dreamed of: She and Cloudtail had two litters of kits, and their daughter Whitewing had her own kits, Dovewing and Ivypool, who played a critical part in saving the Clans from the Dark Forest.

Cloudtail never flinched from Brightheart's scars. But then he knew how it felt to be different, not just because of his fluffy, white pelt that older warriors scorned for the way its brightness stood out to every piece of prey. Cloudtail was the son of Firestar's kittypet sister, Princess. She gave him up to be raised as a ThunderClan warrior. As an apprentice, Cloudpaw struggled at first; he even went back to the kittypet life until StarClan—and Fireheart—gave him a second chance.

Cloudtail made the long journey from the forest to the lake, helped establish his Clan in a new home far from anything they had known before, and risked his own life to save his Clanmates from badgers, storms, and illness—all without believing in StarClan. But he did believe in the battle between good and evil, and he fought as fiercely as any warrior against the cats of the Dark Forest. In the end, loyalty to the warrior code and to his Clanmates mattered more than anything else.

← annoying kittypet son
meets respected
apprentice

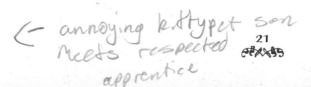

YELLOWFANG

YELLOWFANG

YELLOWFANG WAS THE EXILED ShadowClan medicine cat discovered on an early solo patrol by Firepaw, who would one day become Firestar. His act of kindness in giving her a piece of fresh-kill was punished by Bluestar because he had broken the warrior code of feeding elders and kits from his own Clan first. As a result, Firepaw was ordered to feed and care for Yellowfang in her first moons in the Clan, where she was viewed with suspicion because of ThunderClan's long rivalry with bloodthirsty ShadowClan. In spite of Yellowfang's simmering anger at being treated like a prisoner, she formed a strong bond with the young kittypet-turned-warrior, a connection that lasted beyond her death.

Yellowfang was cranky, stubborn, impatient—and the most loyal cat you could ever meet. Her whole life was a quest for loyalty—to ShadowClan, to her role as their medicine cat, to the son that she bore in secret, and then to ThunderClan after her exile. Yellowfang's biggest mistake was her love for Raggedstar, leader of ShadowClan, despite knowing that medicine cats are forbidden from having mates or kits. When Yellowfang's bitter, neglected son, Brokenstar, became ShadowClan's leader and made the forest run red with the blood of kits too young to fight, Yellowfang's loyalty to what she knew to be right led to Brokenstar exiling her and forcing her across the border to ThunderClan.

She blamed herself wholly for Brokenstar's brutality, and when he was finally defeated during a raid on the ThunderClan camp, she persuaded Bluestar to let him stay there, blind and captive. Just a few moons later, Yellowfang discovered that Brokenstar had plotted with Tigerclaw and some rogues against the Clan that had given him food and shelter. Wracked with guilt, Yellowfang fed deathberries to her own son: It was the only solution she could find for a problem she believed she had caused. Her loyalty to ThunderClan was proven beyond all doubt when she died saving her adopted Clanmates from a fire that swept through their camp. Fireheart grieved as if he had lost his own mother.

← grouchy elder

CINDERPELT

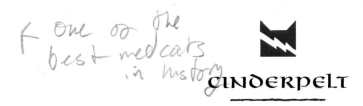

CINDERPELT

CINDERPELT WAS A MEDICINE cat who should have been a warrior. She was Fireheart's first apprentice, but when she was struck by a monster on the Thunderpath, she injured her hind leg so badly that she had to give up all her hopes of hunting and fighting for her Clan. In spite of her disappointment, she trained fiercely as Yellowfang's apprentice and became a skilled and reliable medicine cat. She fought hard to save Silverstream's life at the birth of Graystripe's kits and was always haunted by her failure. Cinderpelt tried to make amends by helping two sickly ShadowClan cats who sought refuge in ThunderClan's territory; this forged a strong, lasting friendship with one of them, Littlecloud, who went on to become ShadowClan's medicine cat.

Cinderpelt didn't have the same sensitivity to StarClan that other medicine cats have had; for example, she interpreted blades of burning grass as a warning that Brambleclaw and Squirrelflight would unite—fire and tiger—to destroy ThunderClan. In fact, those cats' quest to the sun-drown-place saved the Clan by finding them a new home.

But StarClan did not blame Cinderpelt for her mistake. They understood that she should never have been a medicine cat. Her warrior ancestors gave her one more test before deciding to give her a second chance: Led by Bluestar, they told Cinderpelt when she would die and then let her live with that knowledge even though her apprentice, Leafpool, was on the brink of leaving the Clan to be with the WindClan warrior Crowfeather. Cinderpelt went on in the shadow of her own death with such courage and dignity, resisting the temptation to beg Leafpool to stay, that she proved herself worthy of a second life, returning to ThunderClan at the moment of her final breath as one of Sorreltail's kits, Cinderheart.

Leafpool

Leafpool

IN CONTRAST WITH CINDERPELT, Leafpool was always destined to be a medicine cat. From birth, she had a special sensitivity to other cats, particularly her sister. As young apprentices, Leafpaw and Squirrelpaw could always sense where the other was and what they were feeling. StarClan fostered this link because they knew Squirrelpaw would be journeying far from the forest—farther than any Clan cat had been before—and they needed a cat back home to be aware of what she was going through.

For a while it seemed that, young as she was, Leafpool knew what lay around every corner and over every horizon. She knew the Clans had found their new homes when they reached the lake; she knew that Brambleclaw would make a strong and loyal deputy for ThunderClan; she even knew that blood would spill blood before the Clans were truly settled around the lake—and she watched with her own eyes as Brambleclaw killed his half brother, Hawkfrost, to save Firestar.

But the one thing Leafpool did not foresee was falling in love with a WindClan warrior, Crowfeather. Like Yellowfang before her, she broke the warrior code and bore kits: Lionkit, Hollykit, and Jaykit. To keep Leafpool's secret, Squirrelflight raised the kits as her own, even convincing her mate, Brambleclaw, that they were his. Leafpool suffered the pain of watching her kits grow up without them knowing she was their mother.

When her secret was discovered by Hollyleaf and blurted out at a Gathering of all the Clans, Leafpool was forced to give up her role as ThunderClan's medicine cat and become a warrior instead. To add to her agony, her kits hated her for lying to them, especially Jayfeather, who became medicine cat in her place. But Leafpool never judged them, and she served her Clan with quiet loyalty until Jayfeather realized that her skills and experience were too precious to lose and invited her to return to the medicine den alongside him.

SQUIRRELFLIGHT

SQUIRRELFLIGHT

IF LEAFPOOL WAS LIKE water—calm, deep, reflecting the stars—then Squirrelflight was fire. She had enough energy to scorch every tree in the forest, and a tongue that could leave scars in beech bark. She was passionately loyal to her Clan and incapable of doing anything but what she believed to be right—including taking on her sister's kits and making their Clanmates believe they were Squirrelflight's own.

Squirrelpaw was still an apprentice when she insisted on joining Brambleclaw on the quest to sun-drown-place, following the message from StarClan that they must "listen to what midnight tells you." Midnight turned out to be a wise, old badger who steered the cats toward their new home by the lake. Squirrelpaw proved herself to be a brave, feisty companion to the other cats on the quest, demonstrating the courage of her father, Firestar, and the quiet determination of her mother, Sandstorm. For a while on the journey, it seemed as if she was growing close to the RiverClan warrior, Stormfur, but it was Brambleclaw who captured her heart.

Once the Clans had settled by the lake, Ashfur fell in love with Squirrelflight, noticing something behind the mischief and the fire, when Brambleclaw saw only a quarrelsome nuisance. But though Ashfur would have been loyal to the end, he failed to appreciate the strength beneath her impulsive ways. Squirrelflight needed someone to match her fire, not contain it, and that cat was always going to be Brambleclaw.

Squirrelflight watched Brambleclaw raise Lionblaze, Hollyleaf, and Jayfeather as his own, a fair and devoted father. When the truth came out that the kits were Leafpool's, Brambleclaw couldn't forgive Squirrelflight for lying to him. Squirrelflight accepted his anger as her punishment; the death of Ashfur and the shame she had brought to the whole of ThunderClan meant that she didn't feel worthy of being loved. But she never stopped being unwaveringly loyal to her Clan, and fought like a lion in the battle against the Dark Forest. When Brambleclaw became leader after Firestar's death, there was only one cat he could choose to be his deputy: Squirrelflight, his former mate, the cat he knew he could trust to his very last breath.

← Best ThunderClan shecat

BRAMBLECLAW

← a "rubbish" leader

BRAMBLECLAW

THE SON OF TIGERSTAR was always going to walk a path of light and shadow, torn between the courage and ambition he inherited from his father and loyalty toward the Clan his father had tried to destroy. Brambleclaw was the first cat chosen by StarClan to go on the quest to find Midnight, and the fact that Firestar didn't hesitate to trust him sent a clear signal to his Clanmates that Brambleclaw should not be judged for Tigerstar's sins. Though still a young and inexperienced warrior, Brambleclaw led the five other cats through Twolegplaces and across mountains to the sun-drown-place. He endured the return journey, keeping his little band of warriors together even after Feathertail's tragic death in the Cave of Rushing Water, and inspired Firestar and the other Clan leaders to set out in search of a new, safer home.

But at the same time he showed the greatest courage in saving his Clanmates, Brambleclaw was also walking with Tigerstar in his dreams, letting his father nurture his ambitions to lead his Clan, and scheming with his RiverClan half brother, Hawkfrost, to destroy the weaker Clans. Brambleclaw stepped as close as he possibly could to the path of vengeance and bloodthirsty destruction that Tigerstar had planned for so long. But at the last moment, faced with the possibility of Firestar losing his lives in a trap set by Hawkfrost, Brambleclaw realized where his loyalties truly lay. He killed Hawkfrost, fulfilling the prophecy that "before all is peaceful, blood will spill blood," and turned his back on Tigerstar's attempts to corrupt him.

Brambleclaw's greatest challenge after that was becoming a father to Lionblaze, Hollyleaf, and Jayfeather, a challenge that he relished as he watched the kits grow up into strong, loyal members of ThunderClan. His heart was broken when he learned that Crowfeather of WindClan was their real father, and Squirrelflight had lied to him all along. But he kept a check on his rage, stayed loyal to his Clan, and served Firestar well as his deputy. Deep down, Brambleclaw knew that Squirrelflight had followed the only path she could to keep her sister's kits safe from hostility and rejection. He missed her wisdom, her generous spirit, and her impulsive desire to help others, and he wanted no other cat beside him as deputy when he became ThunderClan's leader.

ASHFUR

← a brave stalker

ASHFUR

ASHFUR TRULY LOVED SQUIRRELFLIGHT and was bitterly hurt when she passed him over in favor of Brambleclaw. That was the defense he would offer for his dramatic—and terrible—actions on top of the cliff in the midst of a thunderstorm, when he threatened to kill Squirrelflight's kits to punish her. There was no way he could have expected the reaction he received, which was Squirrelflight telling him that the three cats meant nothing to her because she was not their real mother.

Now Ashfur had an even more powerful weapon to use against Squirrelflight; the chance to reveal to the Clan that she had been lying to them about Lionblaze, Hollyleaf, and Jayfeather. Would Ashfur really have done this, knowing it would hurt Squirrelflight more than dying with her secret untold?

It was too great a risk for Hollyleaf, who tracked Ashfur to the stream on the boundary with WindClan and fatally wounded him. It was a tragic and unfortunate end for a cat whose greatest fault had been loving too much. He was a strong, brave warrior, and a good mentor for Lionblaze because he was able to shape the young cat's raw talent for fighting into powerful, well-practiced techniques. Ashfur may not have been a close friend of Firestar, but that didn't stop him from being trustworthy, loyal to his Clan, and a valuable warrior in the thick of battle. In different circumstances—if the cat who he loved had loved him back—he might have led a noble, well-respected life, perhaps even become deputy and leader. But his rivalry with Brambleclaw, and the love for Squirrelflight that soured so cruelly, put him on a path that led only to tragedy.

LIONBLAZE

Lionblaze

"T HERE WILL BE THREE, kin of your kin, who hold the power of the stars in their paws." Firestar received this prophecy from Skywatcher, the last surviving link to the original SkyClan cats. He waited a long time for three kits to be born, wondering all the time what exactly the prophecy would mean.

When Squirrelflight and Brambleclaw announced the arrival of their kits, Firestar knew that these were the cats of the prophecy. Each of the kits turned out to have unique strengths and abilities. Lionblaze seemed the most likely to play a role in saving the Clan because from the start he was exceptionally strong, skilled at fighting, and as brave as Brambleclaw's father, Tigerstar. Which could be why Tigerstar sought him out in his dreams, walked beside him as he slept, and trained him to be even more fearless and ruthless in his fighting.

Lionblaze rejected Tigerstar's bloodthirsty words of encouragement when he realized that the old cat only wanted revenge on Firestar. He didn't need Tigerstar's mentoring anyway, because Lionblaze soon realized he had a unique ability to fight in the midst of any battle and escape without a scratch on his pelt. As a warrior, he was invincible.

His heart was less so and he fell in love with Cinderheart. But when she learned about the prophecy, about the responsibility Lionblaze bore for every single one of the Clans, she saw herself as nothing more than a distraction from his greater destiny. Lionblaze had to fight one of the hardest battles of his life to make Cinderheart understand that they could choose their own destinies and that being together would not diminish his strength in the final confrontation with the Dark Forest.

⟵ an OP crazy psycho

hollyleaf

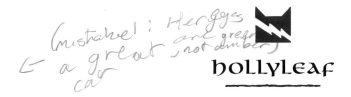

(mistake!: Her eyes are green, not amber)
← a great cat

hollyleaf

FROM THE MOMENT SHE opened her eyes, Lionblaze's sister was the thinker, the politician. She was sensitive and cunning and aware of all the different consequences that might come from a single action. For her, the warrior code lay at the root of every choice a Clan cat had to make, and she was willing to tread the hardest paths to defend it. Even before she heard the prophecy, Hollyleaf was determined to serve her Clan in the best way she could. She started training as a medicine cat with Leafpool, but Leafpool soon realized that Hollyleaf's heart lay in the life of a warrior, defending her Clanmates with tooth and claw rather than repairing the damage done in the battles of other cats. So Hollyleaf dedicated herself to becoming the most skilled warrior ThunderClan had known, training harder and longer than the other apprentices, even her brother, Lionblaze.

When she learned that she and her littermates might one day be more powerful than StarClan, Hollyleaf began searching for the way she would fulfill her destiny. Lionblaze had his unconquerable fighting ability, Jayfeather had the gift of sight in his dreams and the ability to walk in StarClan whenever he chose. Hollyleaf found her strength in her absolute faith in the warrior code, and her courage to defend it to her dying breath.

Hollyleaf was utterly broken by Squirrelflight's revelation that she and her brothers had been born to different cats. Was Hollyleaf nothing but a sordid secret, hidden from her own Clanmates? She was terrified that Ashfur would tell the rest of the Clan and that she'd be driven out for being an aberration, a demonstration of what happened when the warrior code was trampled over. Hollyleaf knew she had to make Ashfur keep the dreadful secret, whatever it took. She didn't mean to kill him—she struck, he slipped, and when he fell into the stream with blood streaming from the wounds in his throat, she knew he was beyond saving. There seemed no point in telling Firestar what had happened. She was being punished enough by her conscience—the warrior code said no cat must kill another—and by her fear that the truth would emerge anyway.

When she and her brothers discovered that Leafpool was their mother, and Crowfeather, a WindClan warrior, was their father, Hollyleaf was overwhelmed by the size of the secret she was trying to keep. The only way she could master it was by revealing everything herself, announcing the truth to a startled Gathering of the Clans, and disgracing Leafpool forever.

Then came her escape into a tunnel that collapsed behind her, leaving her dead to her Clan and everything she had ever known. But the silence of the underground caverns, the quiet, undemanding friendship of Fallen Leaves, and her endless concern for her former Clanmates sent Hollyleaf back to the hollow, to the place where she had been born. The place where she belonged. She fought to the death saving her Clan from the cats of the Dark Forest, her last desperate plea for a forgiveness that had already been granted.

JAYFEATHER

Jayfeather

DESPITE BEING BORN BLIND, able to see only in his dreams, Jayfeather was confident in his ability to also navigate his world when awake. He shared his littermates' courage and curiosity, which led to an adventure with fox cubs that nearly took all of them to StarClan prematurely. Jaypaw saw no reason why he couldn't train to be a warrior alongside them, and he was bitter and angry when Firestar insisted on apprenticing him to Brightheart, the one-eyed warrior, in the hope that she could help the blind apprentice become a warrior too. After his disastrous first battle and a dream visit from Spottedleaf, ThunderClan's former medicine cat, Jaypaw realized that it was his destiny to become a medicine cat and was apprenticed to Leafpool. His memory for herbs and his connection with StarClan made him unusually gifted from the beginning, but Jaypaw still chafed at what he saw as a second-best future, limited to the confines to the territory.

He found freedom by walking in other cats' dreams, which is how he learned about the prophecy Firestar had received so many moons ago. The discovery that he was expected to have more power than StarClan gave Jaypaw the confidence to challenge his ancestors and also to interfere with the destiny of the Tribe of Rushing Water in the mountains. Jaypaw learned from their ancestors, the Tribe of Endless Hunting, that something dark and terrible loomed for all of the Clans—and that the chance of survival depended on him and his littermates.

After receiving his medicine cat name, Jayfeather's destiny became entangled with that of the mountain cats when he walked with the Ancient Clan cats, who had once lived beside the lake, as a long-ago sharpclaw named Jay's Wing. He fell in love with Half Moon and helped guide the cats to the mountains when their home by the lake was threatened. Knowing that he had to return to his own Clan, many seasons and fox-lengths away, Jayfeather made Half Moon the first ever Teller of the Pointed Stones for the mountain cats and gave to her the seeds of a faith in something more than what the cats could see around them—a faith that would be passed on for every generation to come.

I Hate Him

CINDERHEART

CINDERHEART

CINDERHEART WAS BORN TO Sorreltail at the exact moment a badger took the life of Cinderpelt. Perhaps in recognition of Cinderpelt's thwarted destiny and of her unceasing loyalty to her Clan as their medicine cat, StarClan allowed her spirit to return in the body of tiny Cinderheart.

Cinderheart became a warrior apprentice alongside her brothers, training hard to learn how to hunt and fight—and never knowing about her connection to the former medicine cat.

Following an accident in which she fell from a tree while saving another apprentice, Cinderheart's peace began to be disturbed by vivid dreams where she walked through a forest she didn't recognize—and yet it was completely familiar. She knew the names of the cats who lived there and could identify the scents of herbs that clung to her pelt. The images felt as real as memories, but she tried to ignore them until Jayfeather walked with her in the dreams and gently showed her that they *were* memories—from her former life as ThunderClan's medicine cat. Cinderheart was torn between her ambition to be a warrior and serve her Clan by hunting and fighting, and her responsibility to make use of the medicine skills she had somehow been born with. She felt trapped by the destiny that seemed to have been forced upon her.

Only Lionblaze could convince Cinderheart that she could choose her own path. Cinderpelt had lived one life, but this was Cinderheart's life now. And when Cinderheart chose to spend that life as a warrior, alongside Lionblaze, she felt the spirit of the medicine cat lift softly away from her and take its place in StarClan.

← Reincarnation confirmed

DOVEWING

DOVEWING

KIN TO FIRESTAR THROUGH her mother's father, Cloudtail, Dovewing was the third cat of the prophecy, in place of Hollyleaf. From the time she was a tiny kit, she could hear sounds from far, far away, even beyond the lake, and could picture what was happening in other territories. Dovepaw assumed that every cat was the same, so it was a shock when she first learned she was the only one after she helped her Clan by realizing that the shortage of water in the lake was caused by big, brown animals—beavers—building a dam of wood to block a stream much farther up. Jayfeather instantly recognized the potential of Dovewing's gift, but he told her to pretend she had dreamed what was happening, which was something Firestar would understand.

Although she was still only an apprentice, Dovepaw traveled with cats from the other Clans to find the beavers and destroy the dam, releasing the water back into the lake. She forged a powerful friendship with the ShadowClan cat Tigerheart on the journey, a friendship that persisted and deepened when they returned to their own Clans. Even after she had learned about the prophecy and knew about the role she would have to play in the clash between the cats of the Clans and the Dark Forest, Dovepaw couldn't resist visiting Tigerheart at night, using her powers of hearing to keep them safe from detection.

But the looming crisis forced Dovewing to reconsider her loyalties, and she knew that defending her Clan—and the warrior code—mattered more to her than anything else. She found a good friend, somewhat unexpectedly, in Bumblestripe and began to see a future with a cat of her own Clan, rather than the tormented and secret love she'd had for Tigerheart. As the echoes of the final battle died away, with the scratches from Dark Forest cats still stinging on her pelt, Dovewing made her choice.

<- Lel Dopewing

ivypool

key Ivypool

IVYPOOL

IVYPOOL WAS DOVEWING'S ONLY littermate and, like Squirrelflight and Leafpool, the sisters were closer than hairs on a vole's pelt. But their paths began to diverge when, as an apprentice, Dovepaw went on the quest to free the water. When Dovepaw came back, she had distant horizons in her eyes and a connection with cats in other Clans that seemed to stretch the limits of the warrior code.

Feeling unwanted and left out, Ivypaw continued to train hard, even though Dovepaw always seemed to hear and see things much faster than Ivypaw could; on the occasions when Ivypaw did make a catch first, she knew it was because Dovepaw had let her. When a mysterious dark brown cat with ice-blue eyes visited Ivypaw in a dream and offered to train her to be a better warrior than she ever imagined, Ivypaw immediately said yes. Her new mentor, Hawkfrost, led her nightly into a forest of shadows and black rivers, where cats that Ivypaw recognized from other Clans were taught to fight harder, run faster, attack with more cunning than their daylight mentors allowed. Here, Ivypaw shone. She began training apprentices of her own and was sought out for praise by Hawkfrost time after time.

But when Tigerstar laid bare the true purpose of training these cats—to destroy the Clans from within, using cats from past and present—Ivypool, by this time a warrior, swore never to return. Unbeknownst to Ivypool, Jayfeather had followed her into her dreams and discovered her involvement with the Dark Forest. He and Lionblaze saw the potential of recruiting Ivypool to spy for them; to Dovewing's dismay, her sister agreed and risked her life by going back to the Dark Forest to learn when the attack would happen. Despite suspicions from older cats, Ivypool maintained the illusion of loyalty right up until the final charge through to the living Clans. Then she fought with immense courage against cats who she knew had no hesitation about killing to secure a victory.

Hawkfrost cornered Ivypool at last, hissing vengeance for her betrayal, but Hollyleaf leaped forward at the final moment, taking Hawkfrost's death blow and saving Ivypool's life.

BRIARLIGHT

BRIARLIGHT

BRIARLIGHT WAS THE ELDEST of Millie and Graystripe's kits, born in the same litter as Blossomfall and Bumblestripe. As a young apprentice, she was bold and adventurous, like her littermates. She also had a healthy curiosity about Jayfeather's skills as a medicine cat. Near the end of her apprenticeship a storm hit the woods, sending a huge, loose-rooted beech tree crashing down into the hollow. Dovewing heard the tree start to fall and Firestar ordered an evacuation of the entire camp. The blind elder Longtail was killed because he returned to his den to retrieve Mousefur's fresh-kill. Briarpaw chased after him, trying to fetch him back, but was also caught by the crushing branches.

She survived, but her spine was broken, leaving her hindlegs numb and useless. At first Briarpaw believed her future to be utterly bleak and pointless, and she even refused to eat, unwilling to take prey that could feed the cats who hunted and patroled for the Clan. It took stern words from Jayfeather to remind her that a Clan cares for all its cats, including kits and elders who are unable to hunt for themselves. If Briarpaw gave up on life, she would be betraying the warrior code itself.

So Briarpaw started to work hard within the confines of her injury, strengthening her front legs until she could drag herself around the camp and doing breathing exercises to keep her chest strong and clear. Briarpaw helped Jayfeather by sorting and storing herbs, she kept kits entertained, she soothed the elders when they were troubled by bad dreams. And when her littermates received their warrior names, Briarlight was given one too, a reflection of her fierce-burning spirit, in recognition of the unimaginably difficult and unique apprenticeship that she had served.

BRAMBLESTAR'S NINE LIVES; THE RETURN OF HEROES

THE WATER IN THE Moonpool was so cold that Brambleclaw gasped in shock when it touched his nose.

"You'll get used to it," Jayfeather mewed beside him. "Either that, or your nose will go numb."

"Great," muttered Brambleclaw, trying to lie more comfortably on the stones. Inside, he was quivering with excitement as well as exhaustion from making the long journey to the pool so soon after doing battle with the Dark Forest. Grief for Firestar dragged at his pelt and stung his eyes, but this was a moment that Brambleclaw had always known would arrive someday: his own ceremony of nine lives and the start of his leadership of ThunderClan.

"Stop wriggling," Jayfeather hissed. "Close your eyes and wait for StarClan to come to you."

Brambleclaw tucked his forepaws under his chest and let his muzzle fall a little deeper into the Moonpool. The shock of icy water briefly did battle with a heavy wave of tiredness that washed over him. He let himself slip into sleep, but almost at once the sound of whispers made him sit up and look around. What was disturbing him? He was supposed to be sharing tongues with StarClan!

He was still in the rocky hollow that held the Moonpool, round and silver in the moonlight, but now the slopes were filled with rows and rows of cats, glowing and murmuring. *StarClan!* Brambleclaw felt himself gaping as he saw cats so familiar they tore at his heart: Sorreltail, Ferncloud, and his mother, Goldenflower. . . . Soft footsteps sounded beside him, and he turned to see Jayfeather. The medicine cat's blue eyes were clear and bright and focused on Brambleclaw.

"You can see!" he exclaimed.

Jayfeather nodded. "In my dreams, yes." He flicked the tip of his tail. "Not that it makes much difference. Now, are you ready?"

Brambleclaw nodded, trying to ignore the nervous moths that had started whirling in his belly. Jayfeather seemed so old and calm, as if being among the ancient, long-dead cats was as natural as being among his living Clanmates. Brambleclaw looked at the medicine cat and felt a flash of pride. *I raised you as my son,* he thought. *You have done so well, in spite of everything.*

There was a flicker of orange at the far side of the shore, and a cat stepped out of the ranks of StarClan. His eyes shone as green as the forest, and his fur was the color of flame. Brambleclaw felt his eyes fill. "Firestar!" he breathed.

The orange cat trotted lightly over the stones to meet him. Firestar looked young and strong, with no sign of the terrible, bloody battle he had fought until his dying moments. "Welcome to StarClan, Brambleclaw!" he announced.

"It is an honor to be here," Brambleclaw croaked, hardly able to speak through the lump of emotion in his throat.

Firestar lightly rested the tip of his tail on Brambleclaw's flank. "Do not grieve anymore," he mewed. "We always knew this time would come."

Brambleclaw winced. "But not so soon!"

The orange tom shrugged. "StarClan chooses the moment it wishes us to join them. My lives were long and full, and I had so much happiness. And I chose the best deputy I could have, knowing that you would one day succeed me." He stepped closer and touched his muzzle to Brambleclaw's head. "I give you a life with the courage to make the hardest decisions, not just for ThunderClan but for all the Clans. The lake needs four Clans; with this life, serve them all well."

A bolt of lightning seemed to shoot through Brambleclaw's bones, rocking him on his paws. Was this how difficult it would be to honor all of the Clans? He fought for breath until the searing force eased and he was able to open his eyes.

Firestar had stepped back, and in his place stood a cat with fur the color of ripe barley. She smelled of milk and warmth and safety, and Brambleclaw fought down an urge to curl up at her paws and whimper like a kit. "Goldenflower," he whispered. "Is it really you?"

The she-cat's eyes softened. "Yes, my son, it is. I am so proud of you, my love. And so honored to give you this life." She leaned against him, and Brambleclaw flashed back to the nursery, tiny and mewling at Goldenflower's belly, with nothing more sinister than a game of moss-ball ahead of him. "I give you a life for understanding the love of a mother," she meowed. "But then, you have already known what it is to love as a father. Keep that knowledge, feel its power, and use it to keep all of your Clanmates safe."

Warmth filled Brambleclaw from nose to tail-tip, making his legs tremble and a fire blaze in his belly that roared with the sound of tigers. Yes, he had known what it was to love this fiercely. He pictured Lionblaze, Hollyleaf, and Jayfeather, and knew that he would still give his life in a moment to protect them. *Now that is how it must be for all of my Clanmates.*

Bluestar took Goldenflower's place; Brambleclaw felt a pang of sorrow as he watched his mother walk back to the starry rows on the far side of the hollow. Bluestar followed his gaze. "She will be watching over you, always," she murmured. She took a deep breath. "Brambleclaw, you have walked a long and difficult path to reach this point. But you have proven your loyalty to ThunderClan more times than I can count. I am proud to see my Clan pass into your care." She reached up and touched his nose. "I give you a life for clear judgment of character, for the ability to see the value of some cats, and the threat posed by others." Her eyes clouded. "It is a gift I did not always possess myself," she admitted.

"But you found Firestar!" Brambleclaw reminded her.

The she-cat's gaze softened. "So I did." She pressed her muzzle against his. "Tread carefully in whom you trust," she whispered.

This life washed through Brambleclaw's mind like an ice-cold river, making his ears ring and dazzling his eyes with light. He felt a stab of loneliness, as if the life was reminding him that some decisions would be his alone, and the fate of every cat in his Clan would depend upon him making the right choice.

The next cat to walk forward was a dusky brown she-cat with eyes the color of sunlit ice. Her pelt was glossy and the muscles rippled on her shoulders as she padded over the stone. For a moment Brambleclaw didn't recognize her, then his heart leaped and he gasped, "Mousefur?!"

The she-cat's eyes gleamed. "Indeed. Did you think I would always be old and patch-furred, even here? You never knew me when I was young and strong, Brambleclaw. But this is how I will be for the rest of memory." She stretched up to touch his cheek. "I give you a life for listening to your elders, for taking advice even when it is not expected. The oldest cats have seen the most, and there is precious little that is new, even beside the lake. Trust their wisdom, learn from their mistakes, and remember that without them, you would have no Clan to lead."

Brambleclaw's mind filled with countless murmurs and he was buffeted by unseen cats brushing past him on both sides. The hollow was overflowing with cats! He strained to hear what they were saying, but the whispers were too quiet and too numerous to pick anything out. Brambleclaw felt his legs start to tremble from all the memories that swirled around him, and he was grateful when a cat put its shoulder against his side to steady him.

"It's all right," said a deep voice. "Receiving nine lives is always hard, but you are fresh from a battle as well. Stay strong, it will soon be over."

Brambleclaw opened his eyes and looked up at the gold-striped tabby in front of him. The tom's shoulders were even broader than Brambleclaw's, and the way he held his head made Brambleclaw think of the lions that were described in nursery tales.

"I am Lionheart," rumbled the huge tom. "I died in a battle with ShadowClan before you were born, but I have watched you grow, and I know you will make a great leader for my precious ThunderClan. I give you a life to have the greatest pride in your Clan, to honor the legacy that has been left by the leaders who have walked this path before"—he paused and nodded to Bluestar and Firestar—"and to have the courage to lay down your own paw prints over theirs. This is your chance to shape

ThunderClan's destiny. Use it wisely and make us proud."

Lionheart had to stoop to rest his muzzle on top of Brambleclaw's head. Brambleclaw was filled with a warm energy that made his fur stand on end. He pictured all the ThunderClan cats around him, felt their support like a blast of wind that could power him upward, higher than the treetops, to do whatever he wanted to do. "Thank you, Lionheart," he whispered breathlessly.

The noble cat stepped back and dipped his head. "It is always an honor to bestow a life," he meowed.

A lightly framed cat whose pale gray fur was dotted with darker flecks trotted forward. Her green eyes were wide and earnest. Brambleclaw stared at her with a swell of grief. "Ferncloud!"

The she-cat nodded. "Oh, Brambleclaw, this is a bittersweet meeting for both of us. I am so sorry to have left you all behind. Please look after Dustpelt for me, and all my precious kits."

"I will," Brambleclaw promised. "They miss you so much."

Ferncloud's eyes darkened. "And I miss them. But tell them I am watching over them and will be waiting for them always." She gave herself a shake. "I have a life to give you, Brambleclaw!" She sounded almost kitlike with excitement. She reached up and nudged his chin with her nose. "My life is for understanding that it is not only warriors who play a part in protecting the Clan. She-cats who choose to live in the nursery do just as much as those who patrol borders and stock the fresh-kill pile. We raise every new apprentice, feed every small mouth, teach every kit the importance of the warrior code. Without us, the Clan would be as rootless as an upturned tree. Honor the mother-cats, Brambleclaw, for we give you all life."

Brambleclaw was plunged back into the nursery, his nose filled with the scent of milk and warm fur, soft moss enclosing him while his mother licked his ears. The small, shadowed space seemed full of more cats than he could recognize, all bending over him, watching him with warmth in their eyes and purrs rumbling from their bellies. Brambleclaw's chest swelled with gratitude for everything these she-cats had done for his Clan, bringing new lives into the world and nurturing them until they were strong enough to hunt and fight alone. "Thank you, all of you," he murmured, and the cats around him nodded and carried on soothing him until he felt an urge to drift off to sleep.

"Wake up, Brambleclaw!" said an amused voice.

Brambleclaw blinked open his eyes and saw a dark gray she-cat standing in front of him. Her blue eyes reflected the stars as she watched him. "Cinderpelt!" Brambleclaw exclaimed.

The she-cat dipped her head. "It took me a while to reach StarClan, but I am here now," she meowed. Brambleclaw wanted to ask her what she meant, but she went on before he could speak. "I give you a life for offering second chances," she announced, pressing her muzzle to his. "If a plan fails, if a Clanmate disappoints you, if destiny seems the wrong way around, never despair. Have the faith to try again, learn from what happened before, and success may come. The best things come to those who wait, Brambleclaw. Trust me." Again amusement bubbled up in her voice, and Brambleclaw relaxed into the flood of energy that raced through him. Suddenly he felt strong enough to fight every battle twice, double the size of the fresh-kill pile, and train apprentices for twice as long as usual, until they had every skill, every battle tactic perfected.

Cinderpelt brushed her tail lightly along his flank, glanced at Firestar, then padded back to the ranks. Another gray she-cat walked forward, paler than Cinderpelt, with eyes the color of a dawn sky in newleaf. Brambleclaw's breath caught in his throat. This was not a cat he had expected to see.

The she-cat nodded as if she knew what he was thinking. "I walk with the Tribe of Endless Hunting now," she meowed, her voice echoing as if she was still among the vast mountains and tumbling waterfalls where the Tribe cats lived. "But tonight I have come here with my StarClan friends to give you one of your lives."

Brambleclaw bowed his head. "Oh, Feathertail, not a day goes by that I don't think of you. I am so sorry we left you behind."

Feathertail flicked her ears. "But I was part of the Tribe's prophecy, remember? The silver cat who would destroy Sharptooth? The mountains are where I belong, but I have never forgotten the Clans. I watch over you still, and I am so, so proud of you, Brambleclaw." She reached up and pressed her soft, stone-scented cheek against his. "I give you a life for exploring beyond the borders of your Clan, for seeing the possibilities that lie in unexpected places, and the untrodden paths that wait to be discovered. You are not trapped by your invisible boundaries. If you cannot find the answers within them, then look farther off. There is always hope somewhere."

The sharp, slicing wind that Brambleclaw remembered from his stay in the mountains whipped around him, buffeting his fur and rocking him on his paws. He heard the keening cry of an eagle far above him, and his pelt felt damp from the mist thrown up by the waterfall. A pang of longing shot through him, for all the cats he had known and lost, for the long path he had followed in search of a new home for the Clans, for the sights he had seen far beyond the lake and the hills.

"I will be with you, always," Feathertail whispered to him as she faded away to sparkling, empty air.

Brambleclaw looked around. There was just one more life left to receive. Who would give it to him? What more did his leadership need? The starlit cats lined around the hollow were still and watchful. Even the ripples on the surface of the Moonpool had stilled. Everything seemed to be waiting.

Paw steps sounded behind Brambleclaw. He spun around and saw a small, black figure descending the spiral path that led down to the edge of the pool. Brambleclaw tipped his head on one side. Could it be . . . ? Surely not! "Ravenpaw?" he croaked. "Is that you?"

The tom stepped into the light cast by the StarClan cats on the other side of the hollow. The tip of his tail twitched nervously, and his blue eyes blinked several times before he answered. "Yes, it is I," he meowed. He took a deep breath. "Wow. I never expected to see those faces again." He stared at the starry cats, mouth open.

"It's pretty extraordinary, isn't it?" Brambleclaw agreed. He shifted his paws. "So, are you here because . . . well, because you're in your own StarClan now?"

There was a flicker of amusement in Ravenpaw's eyes. "You mean, am I a living cat, or like them?" He nodded at the StarClan ranks. "Oh, I'm one of them," he mewed. "But also not, because my life in the Clans was so long ago. I was so happy with Barley, and I miss him so much." His gaze clouded. "But I see him still, in our home of hay, and I know it won't be long before he is with me once more."

"I remember Barley," meowed Brambleclaw, picturing the sturdy, welcoming black-and-white cat who had given him and his Clanmates shelter at the start of the Great Journey. "He must miss you too."

Ravenpaw blinked. "I should hope so! Now, Brambleclaw, it is a long time since I set eyes on you, but I see why Firestar chose you to be his deputy. I am honored to give you your ninth life, and I am humbled to be part of the new leadership of ThunderClan." He looked at Firestar. "Your Clan will grieve the loss of my dear friend for countless moons," he murmured. "But I know his spirit will be with them all forever."

Lifting his head, he stepped forward and rested his muzzle against Brambleclaw. His voice rang out clear around the rocks of the hollow. "I give you a life for speaking out against injustice, for pursuing the truth above all else. Lies bring shadows in which darker things can hide. Never fear the truth, Brambleclaw, however blinding it may be."

A jolt of light shot through Brambleclaw, shaking him on his paws. His mind cleared as if all his thoughts had been sucked out by the wind, then filled with sunshine so bright he thought his head might blow apart. There was a sharp, dazzling pain before a sense of peace descended on him, all the way down to the end of his tail. Brambleclaw took a deep, shuddering breath.

"It is over," Firestar whispered in his ear. "You have done well." He raised his voice. "Welcome, Bramblestar!"

His new name echoed around the hollow, picked up and cast aloft by every cat that watched him. "Bramblestar! Bramblestar!"

Bramblestar drew himself up and dipped his head to them. "Thank you all," he meowed. "I will do my best to live each of these lives according to the gifts you have made. Firestar, your Clan will never forget you." He held the gaze of his green-eyed mentor. "And if I can be half the leader you were, I will be proud."

Firestar nodded in return. "Go well, Bramblestar," he ordered. "I will be with you always."

shadowclan

Introduction to ShadowClan:
Blackstar Speaks

HEN WE LIVED IN the forest, the other Clans used to say that the hearts of ShadowClan cats had been chilled by the cold winds from the mountains, turning us cruel and cunning. But now that we live around the lake and share the breezes with all the other Clans, what excuse do they make for our skill in battle, our dedication to training as hard as we can, and our absolute loyalty to our Clanmates? Back in the forest, our readiness to invade other territories came from a lack of prey inside our own borders—lizards and frogs can only fill so many bellies in leaf-bare, and it seemed unfair that our neighbors and rivals had rabbits and woodland birds in every season.

And if our leaders took us into battle, what kind of warriors would we have been to refuse? ShadowClan cats are proud of who they are, proud to fight more bravely and tirelessly than any other Clan. Our first warriors were those who were most willing to take action to answer a complaint, to stand by the proof of claws and teeth rather than fine words. We settled on the outskirts of the forest because that gave us the independence we desired, the freedom to choose our own borders and pursue prey as far as we could run. Carrionplace was a bonus, supplying us with rats, though we had to learn fast how to tell if they had been tainted by Twoleg waste and would give us bellyaches.

Our Clan has stayed pure through all the seasons past; strangers are not welcome, and kittypets have no place inside our borders. Tigerstar was an exception, since he was born and raised in ThunderClan, but if our ancestors were willing to give him nine lives, that showed they wanted him to lead us. We have allowed some rogues to join us too, but only after proving their loyalty and courage. Inviting Scourge and his cats of BloodClan into the forest may have been a bad idea, but ShadowClan emerged victorious from that battle. And now, beside the lake, we are still the most feared Clan, the cats who have the fiercest skills in stalking and fighting. These virtues have nothing to do with the wind; they are bred within us, and will endure for as long as the warrior code survives.

RAGGEDSTAR

RAGGEDSTAR

RAGGEDSTAR WAS BORN IN ShadowClan to the warrior Featherstorm, but the identity of his father was always a mystery. Rumors that his father had been a kittypet followed Raggedkit from the moment he opened his eyes, and the taunts that filled his ears made him grow up all the more determined to prove his courage and skill in battle. He was sharp-tongued to the point of being cruel, and measured himself against punishing standards. It was no surprise that Cedarstar chose him to be deputy when he was still a young warrior, after his daring plan to trap rats at the Carrionplace.

Raggedstar, whose warrior name was Raggedpelt, was respected by his Clanmates, but not particularly well liked because of his prickly, defensive nature. Only Yellowpaw, who would one day be Yellowfang, saw through to the vulnerability that made him lash out. It was Yellowpaw who insisted they try to find Raggedpelt's real father in Twolegplace, but when they went in search of him they met with nothing but hostility and denial. In fact, Raggedpelt's father was a Twolegplace rogue named Hal who had no interest in claiming his Clanborn son. Moons later, an attack by Twolegplace rogues brought Raggedpelt face-to-face with Hal once more—and this time Raggedpelt killed him.

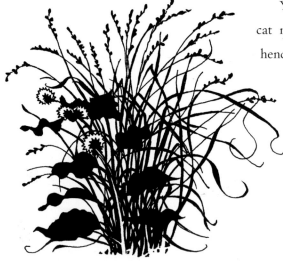

Yellowfang's decision to become a medicine cat made Raggedpelt furious. He couldn't comprehend why she would give up the future she had with him to follow such an isolated path. But it was too late to untangle their paths; Yellowfang soon revealed that she was expecting his kits. Raggedpelt was overjoyed at the prospect of becoming a father, then outraged when Yellowfang said their kits could never know who their real mother was. Only one kit survived, an angry tom with a crooked tail who grew up to become Brokenstar.

Raggedstar raised his son to be fierce enough to fight back against the teasing that came from having no mother; Raggedstar knew how it felt to be rejected by a parent. He was desperately proud of Brokentail and made him deputy as soon as he could, after Cloudpelt was killed in a skirmish with WindClan. But even Raggedstar's ambition and readiness to fight paled beside Brokentail's desire for power. Too late, Raggedstar realized that his son was training cats to fight to kill. He confessed to Yellowfang that he had made a terrible mistake in appointing Brokentail to be deputy so soon and tried to tell Brokentail to train less fiercely. Days later, Brokentail ambushed and killed his father in a remote part of the territory, blaming WindClan trespassers for his death.

↑

Nope

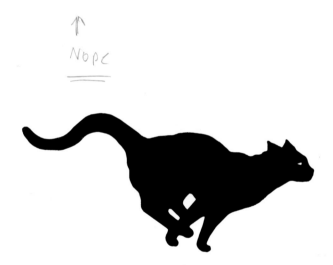

SAGEWHISKER

SAGEWHISKER

SAGEWHISKER WAS THE MEDICINE cat before Yellowfang. She served Cedarstar and then Raggedstar, but died before she had to witness the cruelty of Brokenstar's leadership. Sagewhisker had a prodigious memory for herbs and a gift for listening to StarClan, but her greatest strength lay in observing the cats around her. She was the first to realize that the young she-cat Yellowpaw, who would one day be Yellowfang, had a unique sensitivity to other cats' ailments and felt their pain in sympathy. Sagewhisker encouraged Yellowpaw's curiosity about berries and herbs, secretly hoping that Yellowpaw would ask to be apprenticed as a medicine cat.

But Yellowpaw seemed intent on following the path of a warrior despite her talents and earned the warrior name Yellowfang. Close questioning after a clash with the Twolegplace cats confirmed Sagewhisker's suspicions that, even though Yellowfang had escaped with hardly a scratch, she knew exactly where her Clanmates had been hurt. Yellowfang still had her heart set on serving her Clan as a warrior, not a medicine cat, but Sagewhisker was patient. She knew that this was a decision Yellowfang had to reach on her own, and although she let Yellowfang help with herbs and treatments, she made no attempt to change her mind.

Eventually Yellowfang could no longer bear to fight alongside her Clanmates when she could feel every blow that was struck, and she asked Sagewhisker if she could train as a medicine cat. Without gloating, Sagewhisker agreed and helped Yellowfang find a way to block out the pain of other cats. Soon after Yellowfang became a full medicine cat, Sagewhisker realized the young she-cat was expecting Raggedstar's kits, and she wondered if she had made a terrible mistake. But Sagewhisker believed that being a medicine cat was more important than anything else, and she persuaded Yellowfang to tell Raggedstar so that their kits would have at least one parent in the Clan. Yellowfang took her mentor's advice, and gave Brokenkit up to Lizardstripe as soon as he was born. Sagewhisker kept Yellowfang out of the nursery so she was not distracted by the sight of her son and gave her herbs to dry up her milk.

Sagewhisker died in her den, midway through sorting herbs. She had fulfilled her duty to her very last breath and trusted Yellowfang to do the same.

RUNNINGNOSE and
LITTLECLOUD

RUNNINGNOSE and LITTLECLOUD

RUNNINGNOSE WAS CHOSEN BY Yellowfang to train as a ShadowClan medicine cat. Weaker than his littermates due to his tendency to catch every passing sickness, he was nonetheless cheerful and keen to learn. Yellowfang never did teach him to cure his own sniffles, but he became a skilled and well-respected medicine cat, loyal to his Clan above all else, and patient with the most querulous elder or fractious kit.

His life became much harder once Yellowfang was forced out of ShadowClan, leaving Runningnose in the grip of Brokenstar's bloodthirsty rule. As younger and younger kits were trained to fight, Runningnose had to patch up the tiniest bodies when they returned injured and scared out of their fur. His heart broke for every scrap of life that was lost in Brokenstar's obsessive quest to conquer his rivals.

Even when Brokenstar was captured by ThunderClan, and ShadowClan was free to choose a new leader, Runningnose shouldered the heavy burden of knowing that Nightstar had not been granted his nine lives. Brokenstar still had his final life, despite no longer leading Shadow Clan, and StarClan believed Nightstar was too old and frail to give ShadowClan the leadership it needed. Both Nightstar and his medicine cat were left to lie to the rest of the Clan about the ceremony. Runningnose must have wondered how his path had led him to this, hiding a terrible secret from his precious Clanmates while he struggled to keep Nightstar strong enough to lead them.

Littlecloud was Runningnose's apprentice. Born during Brokenstar's rule, he was forced into warrior training when he was just three moons old. After already being a warrior, he was inspired to become a medicine cat after being rescued by Cinderpelt of ThunderClan during ShadowClan's Great Sickness. Disease from the rats at Carrionplace brought a different kind of death to ShadowClan, and Littlecloud escaped with Whitethroat into ThunderClan territory. Cinderpelt took pity on them and kept them hidden from passing patrols while she treated their sickness. They were eventually chased back to ShadowClan, where Littlecloud turned away from his warrior status to become a medicine cat.

Cinderpelt's kind deed was rewarded by a fair and peaceful medicine cat in ShadowClan for many, many moons. Littlecloud was always willing to share herbs and experience with ThunderClan and watched out for blind Jayfeather on his first independent journeys to the Moonpool. He was devastated when his apprentice, Flametail, drowned after falling through ice on the lake, but unlike his Clanmates, he didn't blame Jayfeather for failing to save him. For Littlecloud, everything was a test of his faith in StarClan, and that never faltered throughout his long life.

BROKENSTAR

BROKENSTAR

BORN IN SECRET TO the ShadowClan medicine cat Yellowfang and raised by Lizardstripe, a queen who had no wish to nurse an extra mouth at her belly, Brokenstar walked a twisted path from the start. From the moment he opened his eyes, he was determined to prove to his Clanmates that he was stronger, braver, and more ferocious than they could ever be. Unflinchingly loyal to his Clan and the warrior code, he quickly became deputy to the leader, his father, Raggedstar—and then killed Raggedstar in order to become leader himself, despite knowing that he was sending his own father to StarClan.

When he stood at the head of ShadowClan, Brokenstar oversaw a reign of terror, unleashing attacks on WindClan and training the smallest kits to fight in the thick of battle. When Yellowfang could no longer bear to treat the wounds on cats who should still have been in the nursery, she spoke out against this practice and was exiled from the Clan. Brokenstar continued his bloodthirsty leadership, driving out WindClan and setting his sights on taking over ThunderClan territory too. But he overextended himself—and underestimated his neighbors—and ended up blind and captive in the ThunderClan camp. Yellowfang grudgingly cared for him, still without telling him the truth about his birth.

When Brokenstar plotted with Tigerstar to launch an attack on ThunderClan from within, Yellowfang took it upon herself to end her son's bloodstained life. Feeding him deathberries, she told him exactly who had kitted him, and how he had brought his destruction upon himself.

Brokenstar continued to rage against the Clans from the Dark Forest, joining with Tigerstar to recruit discontented cats in their dreams. In the final, desperate battle, Yellowfang came from StarClan to obliterate her only son, breaking his neck and sending him out of the Clans forever.

NIGHTSTAR

NIGHTSTAR

As A WARRIOR, NIGHTSTAR, then known as Nightpelt, was dedicated, thoughtful, and well respected. Cedarstar appointed him as mentor to Brokenpaw, hoping that Nightpelt's gentle approach would soften some of the angry young cat's impulses. Brokenpaw had no patience with a warrior that he saw as weak and cowardly, and sought training from Raggedpelt instead. Nightpelt retired to the elders' den soon after Brokentail became a warrior and prepared to live out his days peacefully. But Brokenstar's bloodthirsty rule, and the death of kits too young to be forced into battle, stirred Nightpelt to action.

When Brokenstar was captured by ThunderClan, Nightpelt put himself forward as ShadowClan's new leader. He went to the Moonstone with the medicine cat, Runningnose, where both cats were dismayed to learn that StarClan regarded Brokenstar as the ShadowClan leader still, and thus would not give Nightstar nine lives. It was perhaps Nightstar's greatest moment of courage that he was prepared to lie to his Clanmates and tell them that StarClan approved of his leadership, in order to save them from any further influence from that dark-hearted cat.

Nightstar tried to steer his Clan into a time of peace and recovery, but age and ill health caught up with him and he died after just a few seasons. A bout of greencough stole his single life, leaving ShadowClan lost and leaderless, and ready for Tigerstar.

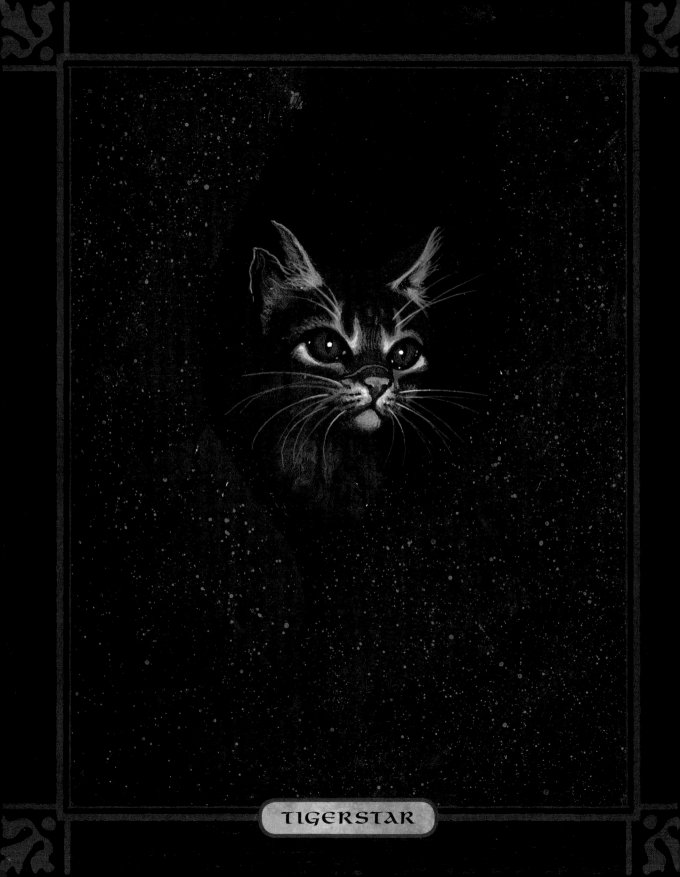

TIGERSTAR

TIGERSTAR

IGERSTAR WAS BORN IN ThunderClan, son of Pinestar and Leopardfoot. Soon after Tigerkit was born, his father left the Clan to take refuge in the life of a kittypet. The shame of this stayed with Tigerstar for all his life and beyond, and his pelt burned with the need to prove his own loyalty, with the warrior code running through his veins. Mentored by the cruel and ambitious Thistleclaw, young Tigerpaw, whose warrior name would be Tigerclaw, wanted to be the greatest warrior his Clan had seen. A skirmish with a young stray kittypet—which Tigerpaw won easily—fueled his hunger for victory. In a clash over Sunningrocks with RiverClan, Tigerclaw saw his chance to kill the ThunderClan deputy, Redtail, and blame it on their rivals. Bluestar eventually made Tigerclaw deputy as he had hoped, but by then her attention had turned to the new arrival in the Clan, a former kittypet named Firepaw, who seemed to be taking the place in Bluestar's confidence that Tigerclaw sought for himself.

As Bluestar declined into old age, Tigerclaw decided he had to hasten his promotion to leader. He tried to lure Bluestar to the Thunderpath but a young apprentice named Cinderpaw came in her place and was badly injured by a passing monster. Increasingly desperate, Tigerclaw plotted with rogues that had once belonged to ShadowClan, and with Brokenstar, the former leader of ShadowClan now held captive by Bluestar, to launch a direct attack on the ThunderClan camp. The attackers were defeated and Tigerclaw was banished from the territory forever. He left swearing vengeance, and found it by joining up with rogues and then charming his way into ShadowClan, which was floundering under Nightstar's leadership. Desperate for a strong cat to reassert their position among the other Clans, ShadowClan welcomed Tigerclaw, and when Nightstar died, he was the natural successor instead of the elderly deputy, Cinderfur.

Tigerstar began plotting against his former Clan at once, first laying a trail of dead rabbits to lure a pack of wild dogs into the heart of the camp, and then forming an ill-advised allegiance with Scourge and his violent cats from Twolegplace, BloodClan. Little did Tigerstar realize that Scourge was the young kittypet whom he'd fought all those moons before. At the moment when ShadowClan, RiverClan, and BloodClan were poised to leap into battle against their neighbors, Scourge turned on Tigerstar and ripped all nine lives from him with one terrible blow.

But for Tigerstar, death was no obstacle to his pursuit of revenge on Firestar and all of ThunderClan. He walked in the dreams of his sons, Hawkfrost and Brambleclaw, training them among the shadows of the Dark Forest and urging them to kill Firestar. Hawkfrost, a RiverClan warrior, was willing to do whatever it took to please Tigerstar, but at the last moment Brambleclaw realized his loyalties lay with his Clan leader, not his long-dead father, and he killed Hawkfrost instead.

Undaunted, Tigerstar walked in the dreams of more and more cats from the Clans, raising an army of warriors who were discontented, restless, or simply keen to learn more fighting skills. Finally he led an onslaught of warriors, dead and alive, out of the Dark Forest and into the living world of the Clans. Face-to-face with his enemy Firestar, Tigerstar struck the fatal blow that took the ThunderClan leader's ninth life. But Firestar matched it with a strike that ended Tigerstar's existence in the Dark Forest, and put him beyond revenge, beyond influence, and beyond a warrior's darkest dreams once and for all.

BLACKSTAR

BLACKSTAR

BLACKSTAR HAD THE UNENVIABLE task of taking over the leadership from Tigerstar. ShadowClan was in ruins, awash with the blood of its own warriors and stained by the memory of inviting BloodClan into the forest. Blackstar took a dogged, loyal, and almost unnoticeable path to restoring the strength of his Clan. He had faith in the virtues at the heart of ShadowClan, the loyalty and courage that ran through the veins of every cat. He acknowledged the role of ShadowClan in bringing death to the forest, but refused to apologize for cats who no longer walked among his Clanmates. Instead, he looked to the future, spoke calmly and without challenge at Gatherings, and willingly let Tawnypelt—born in ThunderClan but now firmly part of ShadowClan—join the quest to find mysterious Midnight and learn the destiny of all four Clans.

Settled in their new territory beside the lake, beneath pine trees that reminded the ShadowClan cats of their former home, Blackstar became disillusioned with a life that seemed as difficult as ever for his warriors. Scarce prey, troublesome kittypets, even Twolegs that invaded the clearing at the edge of their territory, were all things he hoped to have left behind. When his medicine cat, Littlecloud, didn't seem to be getting reassurance from StarClan, Blackstar began to question why their ancestors had brought them to this place.

Then a charismatic rogue named Sol moved to ShadowClan after a battle involving all four Clans. Sol offered a different way of living to Blackstar, one in which cats took care of their own needs, hunted for themselves, and lived free from the burden of the warrior code. He told Blackstar that each cat was more powerful than StarClan because they could control their own destinies. The fact that Sol had predicted a recent eclipse of the sun convinced Blackstar that he should listen to this stranger. ShadowClan stopped attending Gatherings, and Blackstar forbade Littlecloud from visiting the Moonpool. He returned to using the name Blackfoot and ordered all apprentice training to cease.

In despair at the disintegration of ShadowClan, Lionblaze, Hollyleaf, and Jaypaw schemed with Tigerpaw and Dawnpaw to create a false message from StarClan. Lying in wait for Blackfoot in a marshy part of the territory, they dug up saplings to fall onto the former leader and trap him while Jaypaw pretended to be a StarClan cat with a dire warning to start believing in the warrior ancestors once more. At the last moment, Jaypaw was joined by two real StarClan cats, Raggedstar and Runningnose, who told Blackfoot that Sol represented darkness and the imminent loss of the warrior code. Stunned back into faith, Blackstar reclaimed his leader name and exiled Sol.

He led his ShadowClan warriors against the Dark Forest in the Great Battle, and survived. The oldest Clan leader by many moons, still proud of his warriors' fighting skills and fearsome reputation, Blackstar would lay down every one of his remaining lives to defend the warrior code.

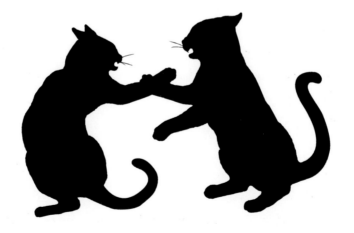

RUSSETFUR

RUSSETFUR

RUSSETFUR WAS BORN TO Twolegplace rogues who gave her the name Red. She came to ShadowClan with Boulder after glimpsing the lifestyle of the proud and disciplined wild cats. Cedarstar changed her name to Russetpaw to mark the beginning of her new life. Russetpaw trained harder than any other apprentice, and quickly earned her Clanmates' respect and the warrior name Russetfur. Despite having left her kittypet life behind, Russetfur was devastated when Raggedpelt killed her father, Hal, in a skirmish. She never learned the truth that Raggedpelt was her half brother and that Hal was also his father. Russetfur dedicated her life to serving ShadowClan and was rewarded by Blackstar when he appointed her deputy.

She had a reputation throughout the Clans for a sharp tongue and a short temper, as well as fearlessness in battle and deep pride in ShadowClan. She played a vital role in helping establish the new territory beside the lake when she took on the troublesome kittypets who lived in a Twoleg den amid the pine trees. Even as she got older and more frail, Russetfur remained the ShadowClan deputy, keeping younger warriors in line with her brisk words and high expectations. She was killed by Lionblaze in a battle over the clearing between ShadowClan and ThunderClan; her death was a shock to everyone, and there were suggestions that such an old cat should not have been allowed to fight. But it was the death Russetfur would have chosen for herself, bravely and in the midst of battle on behalf of her beloved ShadowClan.

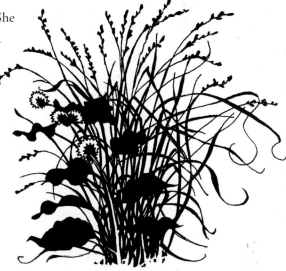

BOULDER

BOULDER

THE SHADOWCLAN WARRIOR BOULDER was born and raised in Twolegplace. He first encountered cats from the forest when Yellowpaw and Raggedpelt visited Twolegplace looking for Raggedpelt's father. Even then, Boulder was full of curiosity about the mysterious wild cats. Later, he took part in a skirmish with ShadowClan cats after one of their patrols caught Twolegplace cats stealing prey. The ShadowClan warriors were victorious, and Boulder had nothing but admiration for the way they had fought: in particular, the fact that the Clan cats could have killed their rivals, but chose not to. He was intrigued by this warrior code that brought with it honor, dignity, and fiercely honed battle skills.

With another Twolegplace rogue named Red, Boulder went to ShadowClan and asked Cedarstar to accept him as a warrior—and Cedarstar agreed. Boulder was given Mousewing as his mentor, but refused to change his name—a decision that was seen as a challenge by the warriors, but was due to nothing more than Boulder's attachment to the name his mother had given him as a kit.

Boulder trained hard, proving himself to be a courageous and skillful fighter, and his origins were soon forgotten. He was an outspoken supporter of Tigerstar when he came to ShadowClan, seeing in the former ThunderClan deputy the bold and fearless leader that could restore ShadowClan to its former strength. And when Tigerstar announced his plans to take power over the whole forest, it was Boulder who suggested an alliance with the Twolegplace cats. Boulder visited Twolegplace on Tigerstar's behalf to speak with Scourge, the new leader of the rogues and former kittypets. But Boulder was too trusting, and when Scourge came to the forest, he killed Tigerstar and took on all four Clans in battle.

Desperate to make amends, Boulder fought with the strength of a horde of badgers to defeat the BloodClan cats. He never mentioned his Twolegplace roots from that moment on and remained a loyal ShadowClan warrior until his peaceful death in the elders' den, in his Clan's new home beside the lake.

TAWNYPELT

TAWNYPELT

BORN IN THUNDERCLAN, BRAMBLECLAW'S littermate and the daughter of Tigerstar and Goldenflower, Tawnypaw was a bright and confident apprentice, with a quickness of temper that sometimes led her into clashes with her Clanmates, especially when her loyalty was questioned. She was horrified to learn the truth behind her father's exile, which had happened when she was still a kit, and insisted that her loyalty was to ThunderClan only, refusing her father's continued requests to join him in ShadowClan once he became their leader.

When Tigerstar allied his Clan with RiverClan and started to drive out all cats with half-Clan blood, Tawnypaw found herself judged more and more harshly by her Clanmates for the crimes of her father. Pushed to the breaking point by Smallear's comparison of her with Tigerstar because she seemed to share her father's reluctance for clearing out the elders' den, Tawnypaw left her home and went to find acceptance in ShadowClan. Even after Tigerstar's death in the battle with BloodClan, Tawnypaw stayed with her adopted Clan, gaining her warrior name—Tawnypelt—and earning Blackstar's trust.

Tawnypelt went on the quest to the sun-drown-place as the representative of ShadowClan, where her courage and willingness to look beyond Clan boundaries made the unlikely group of cats bond much more quickly. She was less hasty to dismiss Crowfeather because of his sullenness and quick temper, and encouraged Feathertail to see past his shy exterior to the qualities beneath. Given that Feathertail died saving Crowfeather from the mountain lion, Sharptooth, perhaps Tawnypelt regretted this later.

Tawnypelt was visited by Tigerstar in her dreams, just like Brambleclaw, but she refused to accept his offer of secret training because she knew her father would never help her achieve what she wanted most: security, peace, and loyalty to one Clan above all. Instead, she found this in Rowanclaw, who fathered her three kits: Flametail, Dawnpelt, and Tigerheart.

Tawnypelt proved that being loyal didn't mean treating all other cats as enemies. She stayed friendly with Brambleclaw and other ThunderClan cats and raised her kits to have the same sense of fairness. While Brambleclaw never completely escaped the shadow cast by their father, Tawnypelt lived her life entirely free of Tigerstar's influence and reputation, with an independence and sense of purpose that Tigerstar himself would have been proud of.

FLAMETAIL

FLAMETAIL

FLAMETAIL WAS THE SON of Tawnypelt and Rowanclaw, and littermate to Dawnpelt and Tigerheart. When he was an apprentice, but had not yet been given a mentor, Blackstar lost faith in StarClan and followed the advice of a rogue named Sol to let each cat choose his own path. Tawnypelt had no wish for her kits to grow up in a Clan that no longer listened to its warrior ancestors, so she took them to ThunderClan and asked for shelter. Flamepaw was particularly angry about Blackstar's change of heart because he was on the verge of being apprenticed to Littlecloud the medicine cat, but all the same, he and his littermates were intrigued to meet Lionblaze, Jaypaw, and Hollyleaf, who were kin because their father, Brambleclaw, was Tawnypelt's brother.

When Jaypaw came up with the idea to fake a sign from StarClan, Flamepaw and his littermates were keen to help. When Blackstar was trapped by the uprooted saplings, Flamepaw was rewarded by the sight of Runningnose and Raggedstar visiting the forest to speak with the ShadowClan leader. This sealed his belief in StarClan and made him even more determined to become a medicine cat. After the apprentices returned to ShadowClan, he was indeed apprenticed to Littlecloud.

He was faced with a lot of responsibility early on when Littlecloud became ill, but Flametail was confident in his skills and successfully treated his Clanmates after the battle with ThunderClan in which Russetfur died. On a visit to the Moonpool, Flametail was warned by Raggedstar's spirit that a time of war was coming, and that the Clans would have to stand alone in order to survive. Littlecloud disagreed, refusing to believe that medicine cat allegiances across Clan borders could ever be threatened. But with Littlecloud confined to the elders' den by his sickness, Flametail was able to convince Blackstar that they had to heed their ancestors' warning and cut themselves off from the other Clans.

As well as Raggedstar's dire prophecy, Flametail started to experience dreadful visions of drowning, being engulfed in black water and trapped by ice. Even slipping into a shallow puddle brought these images crashing into his mind. He interpreted it as yet more warning that a terrible time of darkness was rising up to overwhelm the Clans and worked harder to prepare for the battle that seemed inevitable.

Seeing that the young medicine cat was exhausted and haunted by his dreams, Dawnpelt and Olivenose persuaded Flametail to play a game of prey-stone on the frozen lake. The ice broke beneath Flametail's paws, sending him down to a cold, watery death. He was aware of Jayfeather diving down to help him, and another, hairless, unfamiliar cat nudging Jayfeather away, back to the surface and the air. Flametail was left to drown and was forced to watch his Clanmates battle against the Dark Forest from his place in StarClan.

TIGERSTAR'S NINE LIVES;
STARCLAN MAKES ITS
CHOICE

RUNNINGNOSE REACHED THE DARK, yawning hole below the jagged peaks and stepped aside. "After you, Tigerclaw," he murmured.

Tigerclaw walked past the gray-muzzled medicine cat and stood at the mouth of the tunnel. Dank shadows that tasted of stone lapped at his paws. Above their heads, a sharp wind hurled itself against Highrocks, flattening the grass on the hillside and threatening to dash the few crows that challenged it back down to the ground. But Mothermouth was silent, waiting for cats to enter and have their lives changed beyond all measure.

Tigerclaw had been here before, as an apprentice in ThunderClan. But this time was different. Now he came to claim his nine lives as the new leader of ShadowClan. He had arrived in the Clan after the death of their previous leader, Nightstar, who had left his cats confused, frightened, and still traumatized by Brokenstar's bloody rule. If ever a Clan needed a strong leader, this was it. Tigerclaw bided his time, proved his value as a warrior and hunter, showed his adopted Clanmates that Bluestar had made him deputy of ThunderClan because she saw in him the skills of a future leader. The support of Blackfoot, Russetfur, and Boulder had been essential when it came to putting himself forward as Nightstar's successor. After some tense discussion, the other cats were persuaded. And now, here Tigerclaw stood, on the brink of everything he had ever wished for. Leadership of a Clan. Authority over all his Clanmates. The power to wage war on his enemies.

Sleep with one eye open, Fireheart. I am coming for you.

Behind him, Runningnose stirred. "Tigerclaw, the moon is rising," he meowed.

Tigerclaw looked back at him, feeling his claws scrape against the stone. "StarClan will wait for me," he growled. Of all the cats whose approval he had sought, Runningnose had proved the most difficult. Even now, Tigerstar wasn't convinced of his loyalty. But medicine cats lived to serve their Clan, and Runningnose couldn't oppose the wish of the majority.

"StarClan might, but dawn will not," Runningnose muttered.

Tigerclaw let his front claws extend until they caught the moonlight. Runningnose blinked his rheumy eyes but stayed where he was. Tigerclaw snorted and turned back to the tunnel. He took a deep breath and walked into the shadows, letting the darkness wash over him like water until he was swallowed entirely. Now he was walking blind, using his whiskers to find the walls, setting each paw carefully on the cold, wet stone as the tunnel began to slope steeply down. He could hear Runningnose padding behind him, the medicine cat's rasping breath echoing around the tiny space. Tigerclaw felt a flare of irritation. Who would trust a medicine cat who couldn't cure his own sickness, anyway?

Suddenly the sound of his paw steps changed, the walls fell away from his whiskers on either side, and Tigerclaw knew he had reached the cave where the Moonstone stood. He walked forward more slowly until he felt his muzzle brush against the icy crystal. Runningnose moved closer, until Tigerclaw could feel his hot breath on his flanks.

"Lie down and touch the stone with your nose," the medicine cat instructed.

I know what to do, mouse-brain! Tigerclaw gritted his teeth and sank to his belly, wincing at the feel of the hard, cold floor. He rested his muzzle against the Moonstone and, in the same instant, a shaft of moonlight sliced through the gap in the roof, turning the crystal to dazzling white light. Tigerclaw's heart leaped. *StarClan is here!*

Runningnose settled himself beside Tigerclaw. The warrior tried not to recoil from the stench of old herbs on the medicine cat's ungroomed pelt. "Don't be alarmed," Runningnose began, "if our ancestors do not come to you."

Are you blind? The Moonstone is alight with them!

"When I brought Nightpelt here," Runningnose went on, "things were . . . not as we expected. StarClan did not approve of him as our leader because Brokenstar was still alive. It was a very difficult moment."

Tigerclaw resisted the urge to claw the ears of the foolish old cat. *Everything* was different this time. "But we know that Brokenstar is no longer alive," he meowed. "And ShadowClan themselves have asked me to lead them. Will their ancestors deny the wish of their living Clanmates?"

Runningnose whispered something that might have been a prayer, then mewed out loud, "StarClan knows our destiny better than any of us."

And that destiny is my leadership! Tigerclaw was in no mood to continue debating with the fretful medicine cat. He closed his eyes and felt himself being tugged gently into sleep. Almost at once a cool breeze stirred his fur, scented with pine needles and a mustier tang of marsh water. Tigerclaw blinked and looked around. He was standing at the edge of a forest thick with pines, lapped by a broad expanse of tussocky grass. "I'm . . . I'm in ShadowClan!" he gasped.

A cat stepped out of the trees. "Not exactly," it purred. "This is our version of ShadowClan."

Tigerclaw looked closer at the newcomer. He was a dark gray tom with a white belly and eyes the color of heather. His fur was shot through with starlight, and Tigerclaw could see the outline of tree trunks behind his misted flanks.

"I am Cedarstar," meowed the StarClan cat. "Welcome."

Tigerclaw let out a long breath, suddenly aware of the tension that had made his fur lift along his spine. *StarClan welcomes me!* "Are there others?" he asked. *I need nine lives, not one!*

Cedarstar gestured with his tail to the edge of the woodland. The shadows sparkled with light as, one by one, a long line of cats stepped forward and nodded to Tigerclaw. The warrior stood and stared. *They have come!*

A small, ginger she-cat padded forward until she was barely a mouse-length from Tigerclaw's muzzle. He flinched when he realized he couldn't feel her breath on his nose, then reminded himself that these cats no longer lived the way he did.

"We have waited a long time for you,"

meowed the she-cat. "My name is Littlebird, and I died without being able to save my Clan from Brokenstar. Now my Clan can be strong again."

Tigerclaw bowed his head. "If you will help me, then I will lead your Clan to greater victories than it has ever known before."

"Victory isn't everything," Littlebird mewed lightly. "Sometimes peace brings greater rewards."

Believe that if you wish. Once I am leader, I will use your former Clan to seek revenge on every cat who has ever wronged me.

Littlebird leaned forward and pressed her muzzle against Tigerstar's head. She had to stretch on tiptoe to reach. "I give you a life for compassion," she murmured. "Try to understand what is important to other cats, not just yourself, and let that guide your paws."

In an instant, Tigerclaw's mind whirled with countless images of cats in pain, joy-filled cats, cats wailing in terror or hissing with fury. He staggered, overwhelmed by the emotions that poured into him from all sides, and deafened by the noise inside his world.

"Be strong, Tigerclaw," Littlebird whispered. "It takes more courage than you know to feel what other cats do."

Tigerclaw straightened up. *If I am the leader of my Clan, and my word is law, why should I concern myself with what my Clanmates think? My duty is to lead them; theirs is to follow.* "Thank you, Littlebird," he meowed out loud.

The ferns behind Littlebird stirred and a tiny shape slipped out. Not much bigger than a newborn kit, with a black-and-white pelt that glowed in the half-light, the cat trotted up to Tigerclaw and craned its neck to look up at him. "I am Badgerfang!" he squeaked.

Tigerclaw snorted. "Are you sure? You're the smallest warrior I've ever seen!"

There was a flash of anger in the little cat's eyes that belied his fragile size. "I died as Badgerpaw when I was four moons old. Brokenstar forced me and my littermates to fight in battles before we should even have become apprentices. But I fought bravely and gave my life to save my Clan. Because of that, my mentor, Flintfang, said I could choose my warrior name."

Tigerclaw nodded. "Fine. So what life can you give me?"

Badgerfang blinked. "Be patient," he warned. "Your lives will come as we wish to give them, not as you wish to receive them." He took a step closer and stretched up until his muzzle brushed Tigerclaw's chin. "I give you a life for training your young cats wisely. Train them when they are strong enough to survive their first battle, and encourage them to listen to many cats, including the elders, to learn the most from their Clanmates' histories."

Tigerclaw felt a rush of warmth flood through him, filled with the chattering voices of tiny kits. He recognized his own eagerness to leave the nursery and start training, and he curled his lip with amusement. *Oh, I will train my young Clanmates,* he vowed. *They will soon know they belong to the most powerful Clan in the forest and deserve nothing but victory in every battle!*

Badgerfang trotted away, casting a shadow no bigger than Tigerclaw's front paw, and another cat stood before him. Tigerclaw stared in disbelief at the tall, ginger cat who fathered him. "Pinestar!" he breathed.

The red-furred tom nodded. "Yes, although that is not the name I had when I died."

Tigerclaw felt his claws unsheathe and sink into the soft earth. "Because you were a *kit-typet*," he snarled.

"That was my choice for my final life," Pinestar agreed. "But I walk with our ancestors for tonight to give you a life for being aware of what goes on beyond Clan borders. There are good cats everywhere, Tigerclaw. Do not forget that." He leaned forward and brushed Tigerclaw's nose with his own.

A flurry of images flashed into Tigerclaw's mind, of green fields, lazy swollen rivers, Twolegplaces made of hard red stone, crisscrossed with Thunderpaths and humming with the sound of monsters. He shook his head to clear it. "I will be loyal to my Clanmates above all others," he growled.

Pinestar inclined his head. "The warrior code demands nothing less. But do not assume that every other cat is an enemy or unable to help you in some way." He turned to leave, then looked back. "I am proud of you, my son," he mewed. "When I left the forest, I thought I would never see you again. But here you are, leader of ShadowClan. Perhaps not the choice I would have made," he added wryly, "but you have traveled a hard path to get here, and you deserve your reward."

And I did it all without you, Tigerclaw hissed inside his mind. His pelt prickled at the thought that his father—the treacherous warrior-turned-kittypet—dared give him—loyal to the last, nothing but warrior blood running in his veins—one of his lives. *I won't mind losing that one in battle,* he thought.

The next cat to face him was a small, pale gray she-cat that Tigerclaw didn't recognize. As if reading his thoughts, she meowed, "You won't know me, Tigerclaw. My name is Whitetail. I walked in these woods long ago, before you were even dreamed of. But if we had met before, would you have noticed me, I wonder?"

Surprised, Tigerclaw looked more closely at the she-cat. Her head only just reached his chest, and her pelt hung loosely on her bony frame. If he had encountered her in the midst of a battle, he would have flung her aside with a flick of his paw as if she was nothing more than a moth in his way.

Whitetail didn't give him a chance to answer. "I give you a life for understanding that size isn't everything. Strength does not always mean power, and you should respect your enemies, whatever they look like." She touched her muzzle to his chest, and Tigerclaw felt a strange calm spread through him, cold and heavy like water on his fur. To his dismay, he started to shiver—not just from cold but from fear as well. What was he frightened of? He sank his claws deeper into the ground to hold himself still.

Whitetail looked up at him. "Beware the small cats," she whispered, then turned and walked back into the shadows.

A long-legged, light brown tabby came next, introducing himself as Sedgestar, leader of ShadowClan when there were still five Clans in the forest. He was so old, Tigerclaw could clearly see the trees behind him through his misty outline. But his voice was strong and steady as he rested his muzzle on Tigerclaw's head.

"I give you a life for pride in ShadowClan, knowing they can stand alone through any challenge. ShadowClan needs no allegiances, no help from other Clans when times are hard. Your cats will always find a way to survive if you give them a chance, Tigerclaw."

This life made Tigerclaw feel as if he was growing from the inside, taller than a fox, broader than a badger, filled with the certainty that ShadowClan was the strongest of all. Whatever happened in the forest, ShadowClan would emerge victorious!

A ginger-and-white she-cat with gentle eyes took Sedgestar's place. "I am Flowerstar," she meowed. "Like you, I was not the deputy to the previous leader of ShadowClan. That leader, Brightwhisker, died on her first night of leadership, before she had a chance to receive her nine lives and before she could appoint a new deputy. Our medicine cat, Redscar, found a sign from StarClan—the stalk of an early-blooming snowdrop—that showed our ancestors wished for me to become the next leader." She leaned closer and pressed her sweet-scented nose to Tigerclaw's cheek.

"I give you a life for placing all your faith in StarClan," she murmured. "Trust your warrior ancestors, let them guide you when all seems dark, and honor them with your loyalty for all your lives."

Tigerclaw's pelt lit up with starlight, and he tingled all the way to the tip of his tail. There was fierceness in this life, but also the warmth of a mother's belly fur, all shot through with sparkling light.

Flowerstar stood for a few moments more with her face against Tigerclaw's, until a soft cough from behind made her step aside. A reddish-brown tabby pushed his way forward, and Tigerclaw winced when he saw the jagged scar that stretched from the tabby's ear down the line of his jaw.

"My name is Redscar," mewed the tabby. He looked over his shoulder to check that Flowerstar had disappeared back into the trees. "I am the medicine cat who told Flowerstar that StarClan had chosen her as our leader. But you need to know something: I faked that sign. I picked the snowdrop, severed the blossom, placed the stalk where I could find it in the middle of the camp and announced to everyone that our ancestors had spoken. We needed a leader, and I found them one." His pale eyes looked hot and feverish as he shuffled forward to wedge his muzzle against Tigerclaw's chin. "Listen to StarClan, but do not let that deafen you to your own senses. I give you a life for trusting your own instincts as well. StarClan will guide you, but only you, as leader, can steer the paws of your Clanmates."

Tigerclaw nodded. *At last, a life that makes sense!* He felt a surge of confidence inside his chest, burning like fire and roaring like the wind. Only he knew what was truly right for ShadowClan! They were his cats now!

A dark tortoiseshell she-cat stepped up. Her eyes shone like yellow moons against the shadows behind. "I am Mossheart," she announced. "I was a medicine cat long ago, at a time when cats died every day in needless battles against the other Clans. The forest ran with blood, and my herb stores went unused as cats died before I could do anything to help them. I joined together with the other medicine cats to create a new code, in which warriors do not have to kill their opponents to secure victory. What would become of the Clans if we let all our blood spill into the earth?" She touched Tigerclaw's nose with his. "I give you a life for mercy, for knowing that victory can leave both cats standing. Your opponent may have been the lesser cat in this battle, but he deserves to live and have a chance to try again."

What kind of victory is that, knowing you have spared your enemy for another attack? Tigerclaw braced himself against the tide of heat that swept into him, hating the softness that lapped at his fur, closing his mind to the images of bleeding, maimed warriors that flooded behind his eyes. *If they lose, they deserve to die!*

He opened his eyes and saw Mossheart looking at him. "Mercy brings strength, remember that," she murmured. Tigerclaw felt a stab of alarm. Did the old cat know that this was a life Tigerclaw didn't want?

Mossheart padded away and the cat that had been standing beside Tigerclaw all this time stepped forward. "You have only one more life to receive," meowed Cedarstar. "Are you ready?"

Tigerclaw nodded. *One more, and I will be the true leader of ShadowClan!*

Cedarstar let out a sigh. "I should never have appointed Raggedstar as my deputy," he mewed. "All this trouble goes back to that moment. If only I had known what lay ahead . . ." He lifted his head and placed his muzzle against Tigerclaw's. "I give you a life for farsightedness, for understanding what the results of your actions might be, however distant in the future. It will be the hardest and most lonely part of your duty as leader, Tigerclaw, but essential to keep your Clan safe. Do not rush into anything. Look forward, and choose the path that leads to where you would want your Clanmates to be."

The life was clear and sparkling like the light from the Moonstone. It danced through Tigerclaw's fur, sharpening all his senses until he felt as if he could see right to the edges of StarClan. Something stirred at the back of Tigerclaw's mind.

"But Cedarstar, where are my lives for courage? For strength in battle and revenge on my enemies?" He heard his voice go shrill with doubt, and winced.

Cedarstar looked calmly at him. "You bring enough courage, strength, and vengeance in yourself. It is the duty of StarClan to give you lives for what you might lack, to make your leadership fair for all the cats in your care."

Tigerclaw twitched his ears. *If StarClan trusts me to win battles without their help, who am I to argue?* "Thank you, Cedarstar," he mewed.

"Welcome, Tigerstar!" Cedarstar declared, stepping back and raising his voice. "Lead ShadowClan well with all of your lives!"

"Welcome, Tigerstar!"

"Tigerstar!"

"Tigerstar!"

Tigerstar bathed in the cheers of the StarClan cats. *At last! This is what I have waited for my whole life.* He looked around and saw a group of cats standing close together, watching with anxious, hopeful eyes. He recognized the former ShadowClan elders: Cinderfur, Tallpoppy, Darkflower, and Dawncloud. And beside them, Nightstar—or perhaps Nightpelt, here, because he had never been given nine lives? *I will lead your Clan back to the glory it had before,* Tigerstar promised them silently. *Trust me.*

The starlit cats began to fade in front of him. Runningnose appeared, making Tigerstar jump. "I have been here all along," Runningnose meowed. "It is time to leave now."

Tigerstar nodded. "I have a Clan to lead," he declared.

Runningnose paused and looked at him. "With StarClan's blessing," he mewed. "Tigerstar, you must listen to what our ancestors have said to you tonight. If you do not respect what each life stands for, StarClan cannot help you."

Tigerstar tensed. Was his medicine cat *threatening* him? "I heard nothing tonight that challenges what I want to do with my Clan," he growled. "You are my medicine cat, Runningnose. You serve me before your Clanmates, before StarClan."

Runningnose's eyes darkened for a moment, then he dipped his head. "Of course, Tigerstar," he murmured.

Tigerstar lifted his head and stared at the star-washed landscape. "ShadowClan is mine," he whispered. "And I have nine lifetimes to make them remember me forever!"

WINDCLAN

Introduction to WindClan:
Tallstar Speaks

THE OTHER CLANS HAVE always been quick to dismiss WindClan as puny and skittish, easy to defeat in battle and the least skilled at hunting under trees. But we are the most closely descended from the mountain cats, the first settlers in the forest who came in search of a kinder home than that harsh, rocky place behind the waterfall. Like my Clanmates now, they needed broad, open sky above their heads and the breeze in their fur to feel truly free. Why should we want to smother ourselves with tree branches, or soak our pelts in the cold river, every time we need to hunt? We may be small and lithe, but we can run faster than any other Clan, and we alone have the skills to catch rabbits on the open moor.

Don't confuse a keen sense of danger with lack of courage. We can see our enemies coming from far away, and if that makes us more watchful, quicker to alarm than the other Clans, then it only helps to keep us safe. We have no wish to invade other Clans' territories because our hunting skills are best suited to our own territory—but don't assume that we won't fight as fiercely as our neighbors if we are attacked. I would rather make an alliance with another Clan to fend off trouble on an endangered border than risk my Clanmates' survival for the sake of stubborn pride.

I had to watch my Clan suffer more than any other when the Twolegs started to destroy our territory in order to expand the Thunderpath. Their yellow monsters turned our home to rabbitless mud, then made our Clan into prey by trying to poison us. But I would not leave the forest without the other Clans. WindClan is one of four and always will be. Those mountain cats did not leave the waterfall in vain; we will preserve their legacy forever with our speed and determination to survive.

TALLSTAR

TALLSTAR

THE CAT WHO WOULD grow to become Tallstar was born to a pair of tunneling cats, Sandgorse and Palebird, who expected their son to follow the tradition, unique to WindClan, of cats skilled in digging and hunting belowground. But Tallkit preferred running over the open moor with the wind in his fur and hated the thought of being trapped in the dark. Heatherstar realized this and apprenticed him to a moor runner, much to the disappointment of Sandgorse and Palebird. But when Sandgorse was killed in an underground collapse while showing a visiting rogue named Sparrow one of the tunnels, Tallpaw decided to train as a tunneler like his father. However, Heatherstar forbade her cats to go belowground again, and though Tallpaw earned his warrior name, Talltail, he was restless and angry with grief.

Swearing vengeance on Sparrow, Talltail left WindClan and set out to find him. He encountered a kittypet named Jake and struck up an unlikely allegiance, which deepened into true friendship when they traveled beyond Twolegplace to the rogues' new home. Jake told Talltail that he could be a better cat by not taking Sparrow's life in revenge; at the very last moment, with Sparrow poised on top of a cliff above a Thunderpath, Talltail recalled his friend's words and decided to spare Sparrow. But the tom slipped over the edge anyway, forcing Talltail to risk his life to save him.

Sparrow told Talltail that Sandgorse died saving his life from the collapsing tunnel. Humbled by his father's final brave act, Talltail left the rogues, intending to carry on traveling with Jake. But Jake wanted to go home, back to his housefolk, and Talltail knew deep down that he was still a Clan warrior who belonged on the moor. When he returned to WindClan, he fought hard to win back the respect and trust of his Clanmates and was rewarded when Heatherstar made him deputy.

As Clan leader, Tallstar remembered his experiences beyond the moor and was always willing to make allegiances across his borders to protect his Clan. When a young flame-colored cat joined ThunderClan, Tallstar realized he was the son of his old friend Jake. He never let on to Firestar that he had known his father so well, but Tallstar always favored the ThunderClan cat, sometimes to the dismay of his own Clanmates.

Tallstar lived just long enough to make the Great Journey to the lake and died on the shore before the Clans had separated into their new territories. With his dying breath, Tallstar dismissed his deputy, Mudclaw, fearing he would lead WindClan too quickly into battle with the other Clans, and appointed Onewhisker to succeed him instead. Tallstar meant well, but he left Mudclaw to fester and rise up in rebellion against the new leader, while Onestar tried perhaps a little too hard to prove that WindClan no longer needed the friendship of the other Clans to survive.

ONESTAR

ONESTAR

A S A WARRIOR, ONEWHISKER was loyal and courageous, but without the fierce ambition associated with most leaders. He befriended Fireheart, who would eventually become Firestar, after the young ThunderClan warrior rescued WindClan from their temporary home by the Thunderpath, where they had fled after a particularly savage ShadowClan invasion. Their friendship helped both their Clans; Onewhisker persuaded Tallstar not to fight Bluestar when she falsely accused WindClan of theft, and Fireheart was more lenient to hungry WindClan warriors than other trespassers.

But when Onewhisker became leader of WindClan and took the name Onestar, he wanted to prove that WindClan could survive without the help of another Clan. The friendship that had supported him from across the border seemed like a burden, a debt of gratitude that ThunderClan would extract from WindClan until the lake ran dry. Onestar needed to win the respect of his own Clanmates as Mudclaw stirred up rebellion against him. His first challenge was to defeat Mudclaw and his supporters—helped by StarClan sending a bolt of lightning to crush Mudclaw beneath a falling tree. Then he began to reinforce the border between ThunderClan and WindClan more vigorously than Firestar ever anticipated. Onestar made it clear that there would be no favors owed, no ThunderClan cats tolerated on the wrong side of the scent marks.

When Onestar discovered the existence of tunnels linking the two territories, he recognized their potential as a means of attacking ThunderClan from deep inside its borders. He ordered his warriors to train underground, to hone their skills in fighting in dark and cramped spaces. Seasons upon seasons of tunneling still ran in WindClan's blood, and the battle was ferocious. ThunderClan won narrowly, and Onestar's hostility toward Firestar increased. But he was forced to unite with his old friend when the Dark Forest came, bringing all four Clans together to defeat their greatest enemy of all.

MUDCLAW

MUDCLAW

MUDCLAW WAS CHOSEN TO be deputy because Tallstar recognized the need for a warrior who was not afraid to show his claws to balance out his own gentler, peace-loving leadership. Mudclaw was fearless, fiercely loyal to his Clan, and determined to be a strong leader without having the bloodthirsty ambition that had polluted the paths of leaders in other Clans. When Tallstar dismissed him and appointed Onestar in his place, Mudclaw felt utterly betrayed. He saw no reason behind Tallstar's decision, except that the old cat had lost his mind just before losing his ninth life. A challenge to Onestar's leadership seemed entirely logical, and Mudclaw was encouraged by a significant number of cats who shared his disbelief—not just from his own Clan, but ShadowClan and RiverClan too. His most determined supporter was Hawkfrost of RiverClan; ever keen to stir up trouble, Hawkfrost warned Mudclaw that Onestar's reluctance to seize more territory beside the lake than WindClan had originally been given would leave the Clan hungry and weak come leaf-bare.

Mudclaw met his allies from the other Clans secretly on the island in the lake and one cold night, led them in a brave—perhaps even foolhardy—attack on WindClan's new leader. They were defeated when Firestar brought ThunderClan warriors to fight on Onestar's side. Mudclaw fled back to the island, where he was killed by a tree that had been felled by a bolt of lightning. The other cats took this as a sign from StarClan that Onestar's leadership had their approval, and Mudclaw had been wrong to launch his challenge. The fallen tree provided a bridge, giving easy access to the island, so future Gatherings could be seen as Mudclaw's dying gift to all the Clans.

CROWFEATHER

CROWFEATHER

S HY, AWKWARD, DEFENSIVE CROWPAW, who would become Crowfeather, seemed an unlikely choice by StarClan to share the quest to find Midnight and learn how the Clans could be saved from Twoleg destruction. He was only an apprentice when he set out on the journey, but he fought as bravely as his companions against hostile kittypets and hungry foxes. Feathertail, the WindClan cat, saw past his shyness and sharp tongue to the brave, thoughtful, loyal warrior beneath, and found something to love. Crowpaw loved her back, softened by her quick humor and her gentle reassurance that he was among friends, even if they didn't share the same Clan.

On their return from finding Midnight, the badger at the edge of the sun-drown-place who told them where to find a new home for the Clans, the cats stopped in the mountains with the Tribe of Rushing Water. These cats were plagued by a mountain lion named Sharptooth. The Clan cats laid a trail to catch Sharptooth and feed him prey stuffed with deathberries, but the mountain lion arrived too soon and Crowpaw became trapped in a corner of the cave behind the waterfall. Feathertail leaped up to a talon of stone that hung from the roof and wrenched it free to plunge down into Sharptooth's back, killing him instantly. The fall killed Feathertail too, and Crowpaw was left with the horrifying knowledge that the cat he loved had given her own life to save his.

He chose his warrior name, Crowfeather, in her memory and vowed never to let himself become so vulnerable by falling in love again. Leafpool, the ThunderClan medicine cat, showed sympathy for his heartbreak and tried to reassure him that Feathertail was still with them, watching over him from the stars and urging him to move on from his grief. Crowfeather had no intention of letting Feathertail slip from his mind and refused to be comforted. But in an attack by ShadowClan, when ThunderClan and WindClan warriors fought side by side, Crowfeather found Leafpool clinging to the top of a cliff, about to crash down into the hollow beneath. His mind whirled straight back to the moment Feathertail had lost her life in a fall—

but this time he knew he could save Leafpool. In that moment, he realized he loved Leafpool just as he had loved Feathertail, however guilt-stricken that made him feel.

The two cats tried to deny their feelings until Crowfeather persuaded Leafpool that they would be happier together, even if that meant leaving their Clans. They had been gone for less than a day when they learned of a badger attack against ThunderClan. Crowfeather realized that Leafpool would never forgive herself if she did not return to help her Clanmates. They arrived at the hollow in time to see Cinderpelt, the other medicine cat, being killed by a badger, just as Sorreltail's kits came into the world. Crowfeather's heart broke all over again, knowing that Leafpool would stay with her Clan now.

He went back to WindClan and took Nightcloud as his mate in an attempt to prove to his suspicious Clanmates that he was a loyal warrior once more. Nightcloud gave birth to Breezepelt, but unbeknownst to Crowfeather, Leafpool was expecting his kits too. Lionblaze, Hollyleaf, and Jayfeather were raised by Squirrelflight and Brambleclaw, but when the truth emerged about their true parentage, Crowfeather was horrified and refused to acknowledge them as his own. However much his heart still ached for Leafpool, he could not betray his Clan again. He lived in private torment, unable to connect with his difficult WindClan son, Breezepelt, and resentful toward Nightcloud because she was not the she-cat he truly loved.

In the Great Battle with the Dark Forest, Crowfeather realized the legacy he had created when he found Breezepelt attacking Lionblaze. He pulled his WindClan son from the ThunderClan warrior, vowing that he would never let another cat harm a hair on Lionblaze's pelt. Breezepelt tried to blame Crowfeather for driving him to find alliances among the Dark Forest cats, but Crowfeather insisted Breezepelt had made his own decisions. Left alone with Leafpool, Crowfeather admitted he regretted nothing—the closest he would ever come to accepting her kits as his own.

NIGHTCLOUD and
BREEZEPELT

NIGHTCLOUD AND BREEZEPELT

NIGHTCLOUD WAS OLDER THAN Crowfeather, and was starting to feel concerned she would never have a chance to bear kits, when he asked her to be his mate. She accepted with the sincere belief that she would be able to make Crowfeather fall in love with her, but she soon realized he had only asked her in order to prove he was loyal to WindClan. Nightcloud was short-tempered, defensive, and far from well suited to being a second-best choice. She stuck by Crowfeather without respecting him or even liking him particularly, but she loved their son, Breezepelt, with a ferocity that came from anger because Crowfeather did not love him equally. Nightcloud coddled her son, encouraged him to believe he was better than the other warriors, and in doing so, never gave him a chance to prove his own worth. Her bitterness toward Crowfeather tainted Breezepelt with its poison—though it's hard to blame Nightcloud when Crowfeather put her in such a difficult position.

Breezepelt was always desperate for some acknowledgment from his quiet, undemonstrative father. He had heard the whispers about Crowfeather's past and was determined to prove that he would never be so disloyal. Breezepelt could have been a brave, fierce, and loyal WindClan warrior, but Crowfeather's disinterest and his mother's insistence that he had to answer to no one gave Breezepelt a dangerous arrogance that was mixed with fury against his father. On a journey to the mountains with ThunderClan cats when he was an apprentice, Breezepaw watched how Jaypaw and Lionpaw were treated with warmth and easy affection by Brambleclaw, and his fury burned brighter. His horror when he learned that Jayfeather, Lionblaze, and Hollyleaf were actually Crowfeather's kits is not hard to imagine.

When cats from the Dark Forest walked in his dreams, offering him a chance to become a better warrior than his Clanmates, Breezepelt accepted. He was one of the few cats who understood the true nature of the Dark Forest's attack on the Clans—and he relished the thought of punishing those cats who had made his life so difficult. In the depths of the battle, he launched himself on Lionblaze, who seemed to represent everything that was wrong for Breezepelt. But Crowfeather pulled him away and chased him off, blaming Breezepelt for making his own choices and leading himself down the darkest of paths. With tragic irony, Breezepelt failed to get revenge, failed to even out the balance of injustice he struggled with every day, and gave his father a chance to acknowledge his ThunderClan son.

heathertail

heathertail

HEATHERPAW WAS A LIVELY, curious, impulsive WindClan apprentice who first encountered Lionpaw when she and her mentor Crowfeather took Jaypaw back to the ThunderClan camp after a mishap at the edge of the lake. She met Lionpaw again when his patrol came to the aid of WindClan after a dog strayed too close to the camp on the hill. The young cats fought side by side, and the invisible, Clan-bound border between them began to fade.

Frustrated by the difficulty of speaking to Lionpaw at Gatherings, Heatherpaw suggested they meet at night on the boundary between their Clans. She saw no challenge to her loyalty by fostering this friendship, no reason it would make her any less of a warrior. When she discovered an entrance to the tunnels that burrowed beneath the woods and the hillside, she realized she had found the perfect hiding place for their blossoming relationship. Together, she and Lionpaw explored the underground world, playing games of DarkClan in the largest cave, neither of them aware of the ancient eyes that watched them from the shadows.

Meanwhile, relations between their Clans deteriorated, with Onestar determined to prove he could be strong without Firestar's help. Border clashes made Lionpaw reluctantly decide he could no longer meet Heatherpaw in secret. When three WindClan kits went missing, Onestar assumed that ThunderClan had stolen them. Heatherpaw and Lionpaw guessed that the kits had found their way into the tunnels, and went looking for them with Jaypaw and Hollypaw. Torrential rain flooded the underground river, washing the cats out into the lake, and they narrowly escaped with their lives.

Heatherpaw knew her relationship with Lionpaw could never be rekindled. Their Clans were at war, and she had learned that her loyalty had limits, in spite of what her heart felt. The time came, moons later, when she had to face Lionblaze in battle, and her memories of what they had once shared were pushed aside by her duty to WindClan. But she never forgot him entirely and never found his equal among her own Clanmates.

RIVERCLAN

Introduction to RiverClan:
Crookedstar Speaks

RIVERCLAN CATS HAVE ALWAYS been viewed with suspicion by the other Clans because of our skill at swimming, and our fondness for getting our paws wet. We descend mostly from cats who did not come from the mountains to settle in the forest; those wind-tossed, open-air-loving cats had no wish to live among the close, whispering reeds, or dive underwater to catch fresh-kill. Instead, our first ancestors were those who saw the potential of the river for providing food in every season—food that would be safe from the other Clans because of its watery shelter. Our diet of fish made our pelts grow glossy and thick, better suited to keeping out the chill of the waves, and while other Clans scorned our plain, reed-rattled dens, we made them charming with feathers and moss and other trinkets we could collect along the shore.

Our warriors can fight as bravely as any, but we are called lazy and cowardly by the other Clans because we rarely venture into battle. We have no need: If no cats are willing to soak their paws crossing the river to attack us, why should we pick battles with them? The exception was Sunningrocks. Those rocks were ours! When cats first settled in the forest, the river flowed on both sides, cutting them off from ThunderClan and leaving them a short swim from our camp. The river changed direction, giving ThunderClan dry-paw access to the rocks, and those greedy cats instantly claimed them as their own. More blood was shed trying to take them back than I care to remember. Sunningrocks was won and lost, won and lost, every season until we finally left the forest.

Now every Clan lives beside water, although we are still the only cats that swim for our prey. At first we settled on the island, but when StarClan sent the tree-bridge, it was claimed as our new Gathering place, so we have made our territory around a stream that flows into the lake. We have been threatened by curious Twoleg kits and a poisonous pool, but RiverClan quietly endures, taking pride in our independence and our strong-swimming cats.

CROOKEDSTAR

CROOKEDSTAR

WHEN CROOKEDSTAR WAS BORN, he was called Stormkit, but a fall while playing broke his jaw and his mother, Rainflower, renamed him. It seemed to Crookedkit that his mother never recovered from the disappointment of having a disfigured son. She showered attention on his brother, Oakkit, instead, leaving Crookedkit restless and discontent. He left the Clan when he was still a kit and lived with farm cats instead, learning to hunt through fields of wheat, free from the warrior code. But deep down, he was still a Clan cat, and he returned home, was given the apprentice name Crookedpaw, and eventually earned the warrior name Crookedjaw.

In his dreams, he walked with Mapleshade, a cat with revenge in her heart, who let him assume she was from StarClan although she was confined to the Dark Forest. She agreed to make him the most powerful RiverClan warrior of all, if he vowed that nothing would ever be more important to him than his Clan. Crookedpaw could see no trickery in this and made the promise. Mapleshade trained him hard, honed his skills, but also expected Crookedpaw to stand by and watch as, one by one, the cats he loved most were taken away from him.

Crookedjaw proved his worth many times over with his skill at hunting on land and in the river. He never seemed to be able to do enough to please his mother, but he soon won the affection of his denmate Willowbreeze. Mapleshade tested him by luring a Twoleg kit to Willowbreeze, allowing her to be captured and taken back to Twolegplace. Crookedjaw rescued her with the help of her sister, Graypool—and he knew exactly what Mapleshade had done. He was beginning to realize that he had made a terrible promise that would leave him isolated in the midst of the Clan, but Mapleshade would not release him.

A stray dog in the RiverClan camp sent Crookedjaw racing to help, but he was faced with the dreadful choice of saving his Clanmates or rescuing his mother, who had been knocked into the river. Urged on by Mapleshade, Crookedjaw went to help the other warriors, and Rainflower died. Crookedjaw never forgot the moment when he lost his mother, and with her, the chance of ever winning her love.

When Shellheart retired from Clan deputy, the broken jaws of a pike on the fresh-kill pile predicted that Crookedjaw should take his place, despite being so young. Mapleshade took the credit for damaging the fish, and that night Crookedjaw finally realized that he was being trained among Dark Forest warriors and dissatisfied, angry cats from other Clans, including Thistleclaw of ThunderClan. Horrified that he was being asked to kill to secure victory—against the warrior code—Crookedjaw vowed never to return.

But Mapleshade reminded him of the promise he had made, and slowly Crookedjaw's world fell apart. His brother, Oakheart, fell in love with Bluefur, a ThunderClan warrior, and compromised his loyalty to RiverClan. An expedition to hunt rats in a nearby barn, suggested by Crookedjaw, led to the death of Hailstar, plunging Crookedstar too soon into leadership. And then greencough took Willowbreeze and two of their new-kitted daughters, leaving just one, Silverkit, for Crookedstar to raise alone.

For a while Crookedstar thought Mapleshade's curse had lifted, but his daughter Silverstream fell in love with Graystripe, a ThunderClan warrior, and died giving birth to his kits on the other side of the river, in the shadow of Sunningrocks. Thanks to Mapleshade, Crookedstar had achieved everything he had ever wanted—and lost everything that mattered. It is to his credit that he hid so much of his private torment and was regarded as a strong, fair-minded leader throughout the forest.

MAPLESHADE

MAPLESHADE

ORN IN THUNDERCLAN, MAPLESHADE was a keen and loyal apprentice, and a bold, skillful warrior. Her single-minded pursuit of the warrior code, and the courage with which she faced every enemy—cat, fox, or badger—stirred up whispers among her Clanmates that she would soon be deputy, and then leader. Mapleshade reveled in their admiration and burned inside with ambition.

But then she made the tragic mistake of falling in love with a RiverClan warrior named Appledusk. She managed to keep their relationship a secret, creeping out at night to meet him beside the river, until the moment she gave birth. None of her Clanmates stepped forward as the father of her kits, and the medicine cat recognized the proud, handsome RiverClan warrior instantly in the shape of the tiny heads and the way they held their stubby tails.

Mapleshade was cast out by her Clanmates, banished for betraying ThunderClan and the warrior code. In desperation, Mapleshade tried to swim across the river with her kits, to seek refuge in their father's Clan. But the river was swollen from leaf-fall rain, and her kits were swept away. Mapleshade almost drowned trying to save them, but they were already gone, whisked out of her grasp like sodden little leaves. She made it to the other side, but to her horror, Appledusk blamed her when he learned what had happened. He wanted nothing more to do with her, and RiverClan refused to let her stay, not even for one night.

Cast out by the one cat she loved, and by the Clan she had hoped would give her shelter, Mapleshade became a rogue. Her hatred for RiverClan and ThunderClan festered and, unable to get revenge while she was alive, she plotted against them when she walked in the shadows of the Dark Forest. When she saw young Crookedkit—rejected by his mother, cut off from his Clanmates, restless with unfocused ambition—she pounced. She promised to make all his hopes come true in return for one thing: that he would hold his Clan more precious than anything else in the world. Crookedkit agreed, not seeing that loyalty to an entire Clan was not the same as loving a single cat.

With the future RiverClan leader in her thrall, Mapleshade trained him to become the warrior she had been, while steadily stealing everything he loved most. She made him watch his mother drown, his brother fall in love with a ThunderClan cat, and his mate and daughters die of greencough. When his remaining daughter, Silverstream, fell in love with Graystripe and died giving birth to their kits on ThunderClan soil, Mapleshade rejoiced. Now another cat knew what it was to suffer the agonies of risking everything for love—and losing.

When the Clans moved to the lake, Mapleshade followed and plotted with the other Dark Forest cats to use discontented warriors in the living Clans in the greatest battle of all. Mapleshade could never make the Clans suffer enough for what had been done to her.

SILVERSTREAM

SILVERSTREAM

As Crookedstar's only surviving daughter, with her mother Willowbreeze lost soon after giving birth, Silverstream was a feisty, headstrong young cat who could bend her father to her will with little effort. But her impulsive nature was tempered by gentleness inherited from her mother, and she was loved by all her Clanmates. Silverstream was a RiverClan warrior through and through, with freshwater running in her veins, and she never intended to fall in love with a ThunderClan warrior. She saved Graystripe from drowning not with any romantic notions, but because RiverClan cats were not in the habit of letting dead cats pollute their source of prey.

When Graystripe begged to see her again, Silverstream agreed out of curiosity. Her fondness for the ThunderClan warrior grew in spite of all her instincts to stay loyal to her Clan. When they met in secret, it felt as if she were walking on thorns, and fish stuck in her throat when she returned to her Clanmates at the fresh-kill pile. But she could not deny the pull of her heart, and when she discovered she was expecting Graystripe's kits, her fears were balanced by joy that she would raise a new generation for him.

Tragically she bled to death giving birth at the foot of Sunningrocks, desperately trying to reach her mate. It is hard to know if Silverstream would have been happy to live in ThunderClan, closed in beneath trees and out of sight and sound of her beloved river. But if love could give her the courage to break the warrior code, it might have given her a chance of happiness with Graystripe.

Leopardstar

LEOPARDSTAR

EOPARDFUR, WHO WOULD ONE day become Leopardstar, was a young, keen, ambitious cat who was appointed deputy by Crookedstar because he saw in her a straight-forward, loyal cat with none of the shadows that haunted his dreams. But Leopardfur's black-and-white approach to the warrior code meant that she viewed her leader's more toler-ant attitude toward half-Clan cats—specifically Feathertail and Stormfur, kits of Silverstream and Graystripe—as a grave weakness. When Tigerstar took over ShadowClan and offered a way of making the forest pure Clan, with no petty fighting over boundaries because all cats would belong to one supreme Clan, and no loyalty blurred through half-Clan breeding, Leopardstar formed an alliance that nearly led to the destruction of every cat. Perhaps she also hoped that Tigerstar would invite her to be his mate and share the rule of the forest.

She realized her mistake when Tigerstar combined their Clans into TigerClan and made himself leader, then made half-Clan cats fight to the death. Whatever Leopardstar had hoped for, this was not it. But she was trapped by her pride and couldn't speak out against Tigerstar—not because she was scared for her own safety, but because she couldn't face losing the respect of her Clanmates by admitting she was wrong.

Leopardstar saved her Clanmates by agreeing to join LionClan on the eve of the battle with BloodClan; thanks to Firestar's courage, she ended up on the winning side. But she never forgot how close she came to destroying her Clan. She led her cats on the Great Journey to the lake and supported them through the difficult days of shaping their new home. Her experi-ence with Tigerstar had left her brittle and defensive when dealing with other Clans, but her loyalty to her own Clanmates could not be questioned. She died of sickness in her old age, knowing that RiverClan was safe and well settled beside the lake. It was a peaceful end to a life that had been more turbulent and sad than any other cat truly appreciated.

oakheart

OAKHEART

CROOKEDSTAR'S BROTHER, OAKKIT, WHO would one day be Oakheart, was painfully aware that their mother, Rainflower, favored him over his littermate. Rainflower seemed unable to cope with the fact that one of her kits was disfigured from an accident, but it made no difference to Oakkit. He was fiercely loyal and protective toward his brother, so it was a great shock when, on the day they reached six moons, Crookedkit left RiverClan, and Oakpaw was forced to enter the apprentices' den alone. He trained hard, proved his skills in fighting and fishing, and there were soon murmurs of leadership qualities. Crookedkit returned shortly before Oakpaw became a warrior, and it seemed that everything was as it should be.

But then Oakheart met a feisty, troubled ThunderClan warrior named Bluefur. Her sharp tongue and cool wit fascinated him, and he began to seek her out at Gatherings. Crookedjaw warned him not to get too close to a cat from a rival Clan, but Oakheart saw no harm in what he was doing. He was still as loyal to RiverClan as a warrior could be. After an encounter beside the river, Oakheart suggested to Bluefur that they meet in secret that night at Fourtrees. There in the moonlight she taught him to climb one of the four Great Oaks, all the way to the very top. Beneath the starry sky, Oakheart knew he had fallen in love forever.

They both understood that they could not be together, that one night was all they would have. They parted heartbroken but resolute. Not long after, Crookedstar became leader and asked Oakheart to be his deputy, but Oakheart refused. He was still torn between loyalty to his Clanmates and his love for Bluefur. To his delight, Bluefur came to him and revealed that she was expecting his kits. Oakheart began planning a future in which she would come to RiverClan or he would join ThunderClan. However, Bluefur said she was going to raise these kits alone, telling them nothing about their father except that he was a ThunderClan warrior. Oakheart knew he would never be able to change her mind, but he vowed always to be the kits' father if they needed him.

That time came soon after the three kits were born. Bluefur brought them to the river in deep snow, insisting that she had to give them up to save her Clan from Thistleclaw becoming deputy. One of the kits, Mosskit, died from the cold, but Mistykit and Stonekit survived. Oakheart gave them to Graypool to care for, and watched over them as they grew to be strong, proud RiverClan warriors, knowing nothing of their true mother.

Perhaps mercifully, Oakheart died before he saw Tigerstar's dreadful persecution of half-Clan cats. Oakheart himself was killed by a rock slide during yet another clash over Sunningrocks, a true warrior's end for a cat with more courage and dignity than his Clanmates ever realized.

MISTYSTAR and
STONEFUR

MISTYSTAR AND STONEFUR

MISTYKIT AND STONEKIT WERE born in ThunderClan to the warrior Bluefur, after her illicit relationship with the RiverClan cat Oakheart. Faced with the agonizing knowledge that Thistleclaw was about to become deputy and destroy ThunderClan with his bloodthirsty ambition, Bluefur took her three kits through the snow to the edge of the river and gave them to Oakheart, leaving her free to be chosen as deputy instead. One of the kits, Mosskit, died in the cold, but the other two survived and were raised by Graypool after the death of her own litter. Of course, Graypool guessed exactly where the kits had come from, as did Crookedstar, but they kept Oakheart's secret and raised the cats to be loyal, brave, respected RiverClan warriors.

Leopardstar made Mistyfoot her deputy, and Mistyfoot and Stonefur mentored Stormfur and Feathertail. But then Bluestar revealed to them the truth about their birth, and Mistyfoot and Stonefur became the thing that Leopardstar hated most: half-Clan cats. They were briefly reunited with their mother when she fell into the gorge, saving her Clanmates from a pack of wild dogs. Bluestar died at their paws, happy to have acknowledged her full-grown kits at last.

When Tigerstar took control of RiverClan, Mistyfoot fled across the river to ThunderClan, but Stonefur was captured and killed by Darkstripe and Blackfoot—both of whom had left their Clans to join TigerClan—on Tigerstar's command. Mistyfoot returned to her Clan after the battle with BloodClan and resumed her duties as deputy, under a shocked and chastened Leopardstar. Mistyfoot helped her Clanmates on the Great Journey and stayed loyal to her father's Clan as they settled into their new home.

She never forgot her ThunderClan connections, though, and would have been hard-pressed to declare war on Firestar and his warriors. But her half-Clan roots were long forgiven by all the Clans, and she was regarded with great respect from all around the lake. When Leopardstar died, Mistystar became the leader of RiverClan.

FEATHERTAIL

FEATHERTAIL

FEATHERTAIL NEVER KNEW HER mother, Silverstream, who died giving birth to her at the foot of Sunningrocks. She and her brother, Stormfur, were first raised in ThunderClan by their father, Graystripe, but when they were treated less than kindly by their adopted Clanmates, Graystripe took them back across the river to be raised in their mother's Clan. Graystripe soon returned to ThunderClan, but Featherkit and Stormkit stayed loyal to RiverClan. When Tigerstar rose to power and inflicted his obsession with pure Clan blood on the whole forest, Featherpaw and Stormpaw, now apprentices, were obvious targets. Leopardstar was persuaded to keep them prisoner in an old fox den, together with Featherpaw's mentor, Stonefur, and from that dank hole, Featherpaw and her brother watched Stonefur die in a savagely unfair fight with Darkstripe and Blackfoot.

Firestar, Graystripe, and Ravenpaw rescued them and took them to ThunderClan, where they joined their Clanmate Mistyfoot; like her, they chose to go back to RiverClan when the battle with BloodClan was over. In the following greenleaf, StarClan visited Feathertail, now a warrior, in a dream, urging her to listen to Midnight. Four cats, one from each Clan, received the same message, and joined together to travel to the sun-drown-place and find a way to save their Clanmates from the destruction of the forest. Stormfur went with Feathertail, too loyal to his littermate to let her travel so far alone. But Feathertail was not alone; she fell in love with another cat who had been visited by StarClan, Crowpaw of WindClan. To other cats, he was prickly and reserved, but Feathertail saw through that to the loyal warrior beneath and, free from the borders that divided their forest home, they had no need to hide their affection.

On the return journey from the sun-drown-place, they stayed in the mountains with the Tribe of Rushing Water, and here Feathertail learned that she was part of another prophecy altogether, not from StarClan but from the Tribe of Endless Hunting. They foresaw that a silver cat would be the one to save the Tribe from the mountain lion named Sharptooth that preyed on them. The prophecy came true, but it cost Feathertail her life, plunging from the roof of the cave with the shard of stone that killed Sharptooth. She was buried above the waterfall, and she walks in the stars with the Tribe of Endless Hunting, watching over her adopted home. But she has never forgotten the Clans and often visits them in their dreams, guiding their paw steps with the same gentleness and foresight that she showed in her short, courageous life.

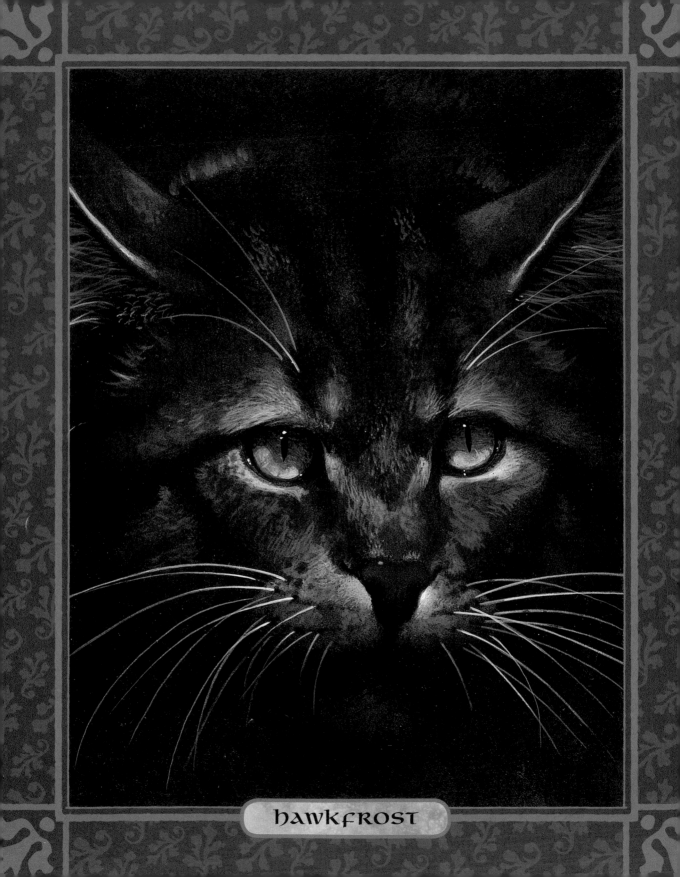

HAWKFROST

hawkfrost

HAWKFROST WAS TIGERSTAR'S OTHER son, half brother to Brambleclaw and Tawnypelt. He and his sister, Mothwing, as well as their brother, Tadpole, were born to a loner named Sasha who strayed into ThunderClan shortly after Tigerstar became leader. Sasha gave birth to her kits alone in the forest and tried to raise them in abandoned Twoleg dens. After nearly losing her litter in a flood that claimed the life of Tadpole, Sasha brought her kits to RiverClan. Although the life of a Clan cat didn't suit her, she hoped it would give her kits a better chance of survival than if they were left in the wild. She came back for them when she learned that the Clans were being forced out of the forest by Twolegs, but by then Hawkfrost and his sister, Mothwing, were grown up and loyal to the code they shared with their Clanmates.

Even before he learned who his father was, Hawkfrost wanted to take Leopardstar's place. He trained harder than any other apprentice, practiced catching fish over and over even though the skill didn't run in his blood as it did in his Clanmates', and was rewarded by being made temporary deputy when Mistyfoot was captured by Twolegs. He was clever enough to know that being Leopardstar's favorite did not mean he was respected by his Clanmates. For that he needed something more . . . such as a sister who was the Clan's medicine cat. So he tore the wing off a moth and faked a sign from StarClan to convince Mudfur that Mothpaw was the right choice for his apprentice.

Tigerstar saw the potential in his ambitious, coldhearted son, and when the cats made the long journey to the lake, Tigerstar began visiting Hawkfrost in his dreams, encouraging him to support Mudclaw in the rebellion against Onestar. When Mudclaw was defeated, Hawkfrost insisted he'd had nothing to do with the uprising.

And it was Tigerstar's idea that Hawkfrost should plot with a ThunderClan cat who was already an enemy of Brambleclaw's to lure Firestar into a trap. That cat was Ashfur, who couldn't have realized just what Hawkfrost was planning. But Tigerstar underestimated

Brambleclaw's loyalty to his Clan leader; instead of killing Firestar as Hawkfrost and Firestar expected, he freed the ThunderClan leader from the trap. Then Brambleclaw turned on his half brother, and StarClan's terrible prophecy was fulfilled: "Before all is peaceful, blood will spill blood and the lake will run red."

Hawkfrost joined his father in the Dark Forest and preyed on discontented cats in the living Clans, urging them to train in their dreams and rise up against the weaknesses of the warrior code. Hawkfrost personally sought out Ivypaw, Dovepaw's troubled sister, and watched with pride as she became one of the Dark Forest's most skilled warriors. Even when his companions doubted her loyalty, Hawkfrost insisted she could be trusted. When he realized that she had duped him all along and had been a ThunderClan spy in their midst, he turned on her. Before he could strike the fatal blow, Hollyleaf leaped to intercept it. Hawkfrost killed her instead and was pursued back to the shadows by a fearsome patrol of living warriors.

MOTHWING and
WILLOWSHINE

MOTHWING AND WILLOWSHINE

MOTHWING WAS ALWAYS FASCINATED by the healing skills of Mudfur, and she had no objection to being trained as his apprentice—but she did object to Hawkfrost's methods of convincing the old cat to mentor her, and she lived in constant fear that his deception would be discovered. Mothwing was a quick learner, sensitive to cats in pain or injured, and well trusted by her Clanmates to care for them. But she suffered from one flaw, unique to any medicine cat in the history of the Clans: Mothwing had no belief in StarClan. The ancestors never walked in her dreams; she felt nothing when she touched the Moonstone or the water of the Moonpool; instinct and experience took the place of sharing tongues with cats that had walked in her paw steps before.

Hawkfrost's threat to reveal her secret meant he was able to force her to make false prophecies, such as the tale about troublesome stones in the river that led to Stormfur and Brook being driven out of the Clan when they tried to settle beside the lake after leaving their mountain home. Because Mothwing was unable to receive warnings from StarClan, she didn't know about the Twoleg poison on RiverClan territory that started killing her Clanmates, and her warrior ancestors couldn't tell her where to find catmint when greencough struck. Terrified that her lie might be destroying her Clan, Mothwing confided in Leafpool, who began speaking to Willowshine in dreams on her behalf.

Mistystar's nine lives ceremony posed a greater challenge, because Mothwing was forced to confess to her closest friend that she did not believe in StarClan. At first Mistystar felt the essence of her leadership was threatened by such a lack of faith, but a vision of a perfect moth emerging triumphant and glorious from a dry brown pod, together with whispers from StarClan, convinced her that she should trust Mothwing to fulfill her duties as she had done for seasons before, rather than judge her for the few things she could not do.

StarClan found a better solution in Willowshine, the RiverClan cat who showed an interest in becoming a medicine cat while she was still a kit. Willowshine's keenness to learn about herbs and her efforts to help during an outbreak of sickness in RiverClan made her an inevitable choice for Mothwing's apprentice. But from the start, Willowshine knew there was something different about her mentor. Mothwing taught her everything she knew about how to heal their Clanmates, but was evasive when it came to interpreting dreams and omens. She took Willowshine to the Moonpool every half-moon with the other medicine cats, but never spoke of the things that StarClan had shared with her. Then, after the death of an elder from greencough, Willowshine was visited in her dream by Leafpool, the ThunderClan medicine cat, and Feathertail, a long-ago RiverClan warrior. They led her to a patch of catmint just beyond RiverClan territory, knowing it would be a precious addition to her herb store.

From that night on, Leafpool walked with Willowshine in her dreams, teaching her about StarClan and how to read omens and watch for signs. Willowshine didn't need to ask why she was being helped by cats from other Clans; she had already guessed that her mentor didn't share her connection to StarClan. But in the same moment, she knew that it didn't matter. Mothwing was a wise, experienced, and skilled medicine cat. She deserved Willowshine's respect and loyalty—and Willowshine vowed to keep Mothwing's secret until her very last breath.

![SkyClan emblem]

skyclan

Introduction to SkyClan: Cloudstar Speaks

SkyClan has the distinction of being the very first Clan in the forest. Our founder, Clear Sky, came from the mountains and chose not to stay with the others on the moor, clinging to an environment that reminded them of home; instead, he saw the potential in the prey-rich woodland, in the dense undergrowth that could offer shelter and secrecy. He took with him the cats that were most skilled at leaping into the air to bring down eagles. This talent was easily turned to climbing trees in pursuit of squirrels and smaller, easier-won birds.

The moorland cats became jealous and resentful, but Clear Sky knew he was sowing the seeds of a group that would grow strong and proud, and last forever.

And perhaps it would have. But Clear Sky could not have foreseen what the Twolegs would do to his precious territory. By the time I became leader, many, many seasons after Clear Sky had gone to walk among the stars, our beloved trees were being torn down to make way for new Twoleg dens.

For the first time, SkyClan was the most vulnerable of all the Clans. We appealed to the others for help, for enough of their territory to survive the bitter cold of leaf-bare, but it seemed our history, our place in establishing the very grounds of the warrior code, meant nothing. Cast out, I led my Clanmates on a long and dreadful journey until I found a gorge carved out of sandy rock that offered shelter and prey and a chance to rest.

SkyClan thrived in its new home, nurturing the flickering flame of the warrior code, until rats came and stole our prey and killed our kits and terrorized us until there was no one left. SkyClan could not suffer two defeats. The cats scattered and the gorge lay empty until Firestar was sent by Bluestar to restore what had once been a noble and important Clan. Firestar and Sandstorm rebuilt our Clan, tracking down our descendants who still showed an echo of our tree-hunting skills, and inviting other cats to join and uphold the warrior code. There were still rats to defeat and the challenge of teaching so many cats at once to live according to the ways of our ancestors, but the heart of SkyClan had never truly died. Maybe we lived apart from the other Clans, maybe some of our cats had not completely cast off their kittypet connections, but SkyClan thrived once more.

CLOUDSTAR and
SKYWATCHER

CLOUDSTAR AND SKYWATCHER

CLOUDSTAR WAS WELL AWARE of the significance of his Clan's place in the history of the forest, and he took as much pride as his Clanmates in SkyClan's strength and reputation. When Twolegs started to destroy the territory to build new dens, Cloudstar trusted his rival Clans to help him survive. Instead, each leader protested that sharing their territory would be impossible, that SkyClan would not be able to catch different prey, that if there were only four Great Oaks in the hollow, perhaps StarClan only ever intended for there to be four Clans.

To his horror, Cloudstar realized that his Clanmates' only chance of survival lay in finding a new home. His mate, Birdflight, stayed behind in ThunderClan with their newborn kits. Numb with grief, Cloudstar found somewhere to rest in a sandy gorge, far upriver from the forest. His faith in StarClan had been shaken so deeply that he gave little heed to the warrior code. Food and shelter, that was all his Clanmates needed. Other leaders came after him, but a savage horde of rats drove out the remaining cats, and from his place in the stars, Cloudstar watched his beloved Clan dwindle to dust.

Skywatcher was the last descendant of SkyClan living in the gorge when Firestar and Sandstorm arrived. His mother had told him tales of their ancestors who watched the full moon from the rock jutting out over the gorge, and who lived in different sandy dens according to their role in the Clans. Skywatcher lived alone, his thoughts muddled with age and loneliness, spending most of his nights on a rock that jutted from the top of the gorge, staring up at the stars. For this reason, the cats who knew him called him Moony and jeered him for his peculiar, absent ways.

But Firestar recognized the truth in his ramblings of long-ago cats, and when the new SkyClan rose from the dust, Skywatcher was welcomed as an honored elder. He lived just long enough to see his mother's distant memories reignite the gorge, and then died, taking his place among his ancestors. But Skywatcher never forgot the debt he owed to Firestar, and it was he who was chosen to deliver the greatest prophecy of all to the ThunderClan leader: "There will be three, kin of your kin, who hold the power of the stars in their paws."

LEAFSTAR

Leafstar

L EAF WAS A LONER in the woods near the sandy gorge when Firestar first approached her and told her about the cats who lived there long ago. Leaf was happy as she was, hunting for herself, occasionally sharing tongues with her friend Scratch. But she was curious enough about what Firestar said to come to a meeting of cats in the gorge. His tales of StarClan, and of cats that helped each other survive the harshest leaf-bares, drew Leaf in, and along with several others—loners and kittypets alike—she agreed to join the new Clan.

With the warrior name Leafdapple, she learned fast from her ThunderClan mentors. She was given an apprentice of her own, Sparrowpaw, and she helped her Clanmates set border markers around the gorge, protecting the territory that belonged to them now. She fought as fiercely as a lion to defeat the rats that had begun to torment them, just as the old SkyClan had been tormented so many moons ago.

A vision of leaf-shadowed sunlight in the midst of leaf-bare prompted the new medicine cat, Echosong, to speak with Firestar, who realized that this must be a sign for him to choose a leader. At first, Leafdapple resisted taking on so much responsibility when there was still much to learn, but faith in her newly discovered ancestors gave her courage, and she became Leafstar.

With the support of her mate, Billystorm, and her deputy, Sharpclaw, she led SkyClan through its turbulent early seasons, fending off attacks from foxes and hostile cats, as well as negotiating a new kind of Clanmate, a daylight-warrior, part-kittypet and part-Clan cat. Leafstar knew this would not be accepted in other Clans, but she was wise enough to recognize that things were very different for SkyClan. They had to exist alone, and they needed to swell their numbers by any means in order to stay strong and well-fed. Some questioned the loyalty of the daylight-warriors, and some daylight-warriors proved inadequate, but Leafstar's decision was the right one, and SkyClan flourished.

Leafstar had her own litter, Firekit, Stormkit, and Harrykit, and rescued them when a well-meaning elderly Twoleg took them to her den. Her mate, Billystorm, realized how much his family meant to him after this and decided to stay in the gorge forever. Perhaps the only fatal mistake Leafstar made was sending away the would-be warrior Sol; fatal not for her Clan, but for the Clans far away that she had never met.

ECHOSONG

ECHOSONG

ECHOSONG WAS PURE KITTYPET, with no hint of SkyClan in her long, fluffy coat and delicate paws. But she dreamed of cats with the light of stars in their fur, and when Firestar and Sandstorm came looking for new warriors in Twolegplace, Echosong was expecting them. Already made restless by her strange dreams, Echosong was willing to leave her housefolk and go live in the gorge. Her sensitivity to the stars and her quick knowledge of herbs, thanks to Sandstorm's patient teaching, made her an obvious choice for SkyClan's new medicine cat.

The loners in the Clan, including Sharpclaw, were suspicious of the soft-furred kittypet, but Echosong was patient and loyal and proved her worth. She saved lives after the battle with the rats, and shared her Clanmates' grief when it was too late to help the brave warrior Rainfur. It was Echosong who received the sign of dappled leaves to indicate StarClan's choice for the leader of SkyClan, and she traveled with Leafstar to watch her receive her nine lives from their ancestors. Firestar knew that with these two cats, he was leaving the young Clan in the safest paws.

TRIBE OF RUSHING WATER

Introduction to the Tribe of Rushing Water: Stoneteller Speaks

THE TRIBE OF RUSHING Water has been shaped by the mountains that are our home. We are lithe, quick-moving, and the color of stone, our pelts blending into the rocks. Even our names echo the stark beauty that lies all around us: the sharp peaks outlined against the sky, the dazzle and foam of the waterfall, the clouds that drift high above us or lie heavy on the summits.

As the Teller of the Pointed Stones, leader and healer of all the cats behind the waterfall, it is my duty to share tongues with my ancestors, to read the signs of moonlight on the surface of the pools, in the drip of water and the wind that ruffles it. Clan cats look up to the stars for their omens; we look down into shining water, sheltered in our cave.

The first cats to settle in the mountains came here from the lake. I wonder if the Clan cats know they have come full circle, for it was mountain cats who went to find a new home in the forest, where the Clans lived for so many warm and generous seasons. At first, we struggled to survive in the harsh and lonely mountains, persecuted by the endless wind and the tendency of our eagle prey to kill us before we could pluck them from the air. The cats began to divide according to their talents, the brave and quick fighters taking on the role of protecting those who were skilled at tracking what little prey there was. We named these cats "prey-hunters," and the sturdy cats who protected them "cave-guards."

Our young we called "to-bes," because they were to be cave-guards or prey-hunters one day themselves.

In spite of everything, we carved out a life for ourselves and found a way to survive everything the mountains could hurl at us—until Sharptooth came, and we found ourselves helpless as prey, waiting for a silver cat to save us.

TELLER OF THE
POINTED STONES

TELLER OF THE POINTED STONES

THE STONETELLER WHO THE four Clans met on the journey to the lake was an old, old cat who had led his Tribe through many harsh seasons only to face the cruelest enemy of all: a mountain lion named Sharptooth who seemed determined to treat every cat as prey. Stoneteller clung to the hope that his prey-hunters and cave-guards would protect them, but when a party sent out to kill Sharptooth failed to return, he began to despair. If every part of the mountains was set against them—from the snow and cold to the creatures that shared their home—then the Tribe of Rushing Water seemed doomed to extinction.

Then the Tribe of Endless Hunting sent him a prophecy that a silver cat would save them from Sharptooth. When the six Clan cats first arrived on their way to the mysterious sun-drown-place, it seemed as if the prophecy had been fulfilled. The gray tom Stormfur was surely the promised cat! But when Stormfur's battle tactics failed against yet another attack from the mountain lion, Stoneteller banished the Clan cats and Brook Where Small Fish Swim, the Tribe cat that had befriended them, from the cave behind the waterfall. Stoneteller was resigned to watching his Tribe perish in Sharptooth's jaws, and he wondered why their ancestors seemed to have given up on them.

But Brook and the Clan cats returned, bringing with them the exiled Tribe cave-guards, and this time it was another silver-furred cat, Feathertail, who killed Sharptooth. Stoneteller's Tribe had been saved, and proud as he was, he acknowledged the debt he would owe the cats of the Clans for the rest of his life.

When they visited again, having found a new home by a distant lake, Stoneteller had grown weary with age, and the leadership of the Tribe, with no medicine cat or deputy to bear some of the burden, had become too much for him. With the arrival of another group of cats in the mountains who stole the Tribe's prey and fought them over every paw step of territory, Stoneteller had yet again lost his faith in the Tribe of Endless Hunting. Because of this, he refused to name his successor, wanting his cats to find a different way to survive.

In the last moments of his life, he saw his ancestors standing around him, waiting to welcome him to the Tribe of Endless Hunting, and knew that he had been wrong. He watched, grateful, from his place in the stars as the ThunderClan medicine cat Jayfeather chose Crag Where Eagles Nest to be the next Teller of the Pointed Stones. The debt to these strange Clan cats, it seemed, was not over yet.

BROOK WHERE SMALL FISH SWIM
AND STORMFUR

BROOK WHERE SMALL FISH SWIM AND STORMFUR

BORN IN THE CAVE of Rushing Water behind the waterfall in the mountains, Brook Where Small Fish Swim knew early on that she wanted to be a prey-hunter for her Tribe. Brook was fiercely loyal to her Tribe, and when the journeying Clan cats arrived on their return from their meeting with Midnight, she was the first to spot Stormfur and ask whether he could be the cat that had been prophesied to save them from Sharptooth. She invited the forest cats to hunt with her and taught them the Tribe's hunting techniques. She became Stormfur's mate when he decided to stay with the Tribe, and later gave birth to his kits, Lark That Sings At Dawn and Pine That Clings To Rock. Brook was a cat of great courage, who struggled for many seasons with the conflict between her love for Stormfur and her loyalty to her Tribe.

Stormfur was the son of ThunderClan warrior Graystripe and RiverClan warrior Silverstream, and grew up in RiverClan. When his sister, Feathertail, was chosen by StarClan to make the journey to the sun-drown-place, Stormfur insisted on going with her—never imagining that this journey would lead to an eventual separation from the Clan life he had always known.

Stormfur returned to his Clan in the wake of Feathertail's death, but felt isolated. He finally admitted to himself that he wanted to spend his life with Brook, and when the Clans reached the mountains on the Great Journey, he stayed with the Tribe because he cared for Brook so much that he couldn't bear to leave her.

But Brook and Stormfur's life together wasn't easy. When a group of strange cats moved into the mountains, Stormfur persuaded the Tribe to fight against them, and in spite of their courage and the fighting skills he taught them, they lost the battle. Stormfur was blamed for the death of many Tribe cats, and exiled from the mountains. He and Brook returned to RiverClan, but Hawkfrost, afraid that Stormfur would be chosen as deputy instead of him, cast doubt upon his loyalty and had him driven out. Firestar then invited Stormfur and Brook to join ThunderClan, but when the Tribe cats came to the lake to ask for help, Stormfur returned to the mountains and supported the Clan cats in persuading Stoneteller to use Clan methods to deal with the intruders. He was a strong and loyal cat who finally found a place for himself.

THE EARLY SETTLERS

Introduction to the Early Settlers:
Half Moon Speaks

THERE WERE ALWAYS WILD cats living in the territories between Highstones and the Twolegplace, in the woods, moorland, and riverside willow trees that later became the homes of ThunderClan, ShadowClan, SkyClan, WindClan, and RiverClan. But these cats were rogues and loners, living separately and independently, with occasional clashes over a particularly tasty piece of prey. They had favorite places to sun themselves or sleep, but there were no borders between hunting grounds, no sense that one area was more "home" to one cat than another.

Until the cats from the mountains arrived, that is. These cats had left the rugged shelter of a cave beneath a waterfall in search of somewhere richer in prey and warmer to live. Scant generations before, their ancestors had abandoned their home beside a lake, finding refuge in snow-capped mountains where food had to be dragged from the sky on eagles' wings.

I was among those cats that had once lived beside the lake. My name then was Half Moon; by the time some of us left the mountains, I was the Teller of the Pointed Stones, leader of the cats that lived beneath the waterfall. We battled hard to survive among the rocks and the snow, but we brought too many hungry mouths to feed in a place that barely emerged from the cold season.

When I had almost forgotten how it felt to have a full belly, and when my pelt hung loose on my jagged bones, I had a waking dream, a vision as clear as the mountains around me. I saw a soft and sheltering place, safe from the cruel winds that sharpened the mountain peaks, with room for many cats to live and raise kits. There was no chance of my old bones traveling farther than the eye could see from our rocky home, but I gave my blessing to those cats who were brave enough to leave in search of what I had seen. When these far-traveling cats reached Highstones, they looked down on moorland, forest, and winding river, and knew they had found their home.

There were trees for the cats who loved to hunt by stalking and climbing, a broad shallow river for those willing to get their paws wet, and a large stretch of moorland for swift-heeled cats to catch rabbits out in the open. Of course, it took many seasons for the five Clans to emerge with distinct, hard-fought boundaries and the shared laws known as the warrior code. But the seeds of those Clans were sown in the personalities of the early settlers, in their differing preferences for hunting in trees or in open moorland, or risking wet fur in search of a plump fish. They fought and quarreled, shared loss and disaster, but every sunrise, every paw step, every blow struck and prey killed drew them steadily closer to the Clans they would become. And farther from their memories of the cats they had left behind. . . .

half moon,
also known as STONETELLER

bALf Moon,
ALso KNOWN AS STONETELLER

HALF MOON WAS A white she-cat with green eyes, daughter of Rising Moon and Chasing Clouds, who lived beside the lake with the ancient cats. She was one of the first to suggest moving away to find a new place to live. When the cats cast their votes, she showed no hesitation in pushing her stone into the circle that meant "leave."

She loved Jayfeather (who she knew as Jay's Wing) and was heartbroken when he didn't follow them into the mountains, not knowing that Rock had forced him to return to his own time through the tunnels.

When the ancient cats reached their new home in the mountains, Half Moon demonstrated her courage in learning new hunting skills, and when she first explored the Cave of Pointed Stones, she was able to read the signs revealed by moonlight in the water. She was delighted when Jayfeather reappeared in the cave behind the waterfall, but devastated when he told her that her destiny was to become Stoneteller. Despite her abilities, all she wanted was to be Jayfeather's mate and raise his kits, not to lead the mountain cats. Jayfeather wanted that too, but he knew that fate did not guide their paw steps side by side. At last Half Moon accepted what Jayfeather told her and took on the burden of becoming her Tribe's Healer.

Later, as a very old cat, Half Moon received the vision of the Sun Trail, which told her that some of her cats should follow the path of the sun to find a new home. Jayfeather had told her that her ancestors would send her signs, and through all the seasons she still loved and trusted him. When Jayfeather left the mountains for the last time, he heard Half Moon's spirit calling to him, telling him that she would wait for him forever.

GRAY WING

GRAY WING

WHEN THE TELLER OF the Pointed Stones told the cats about her dream of a different place to live, the young tom Gray Wing made it clear he would not leave the mountains. He insisted that he belonged in the Cave of Rushing Water with his mother, Quiet Rain, and younger brother, Jagged Peak. But Gray Wing was courageous and loyal, and when Jagged Peak put himself in danger by following the departing cats, Gray Wing went after him.

Having traveled almost to the edge of the mountains, Gray Wing and Jagged Peak caught up with the other cats and joined the quest to find somewhere else to live. Gray Wing's best friend, Turtle Tail, who had cherished hopes of one day becoming Gray Wing's mate, was overjoyed to see him again—unaware that Gray Wing was secretly in love with Bright Stream, who loved his brother, Clear Sky.

No cat expected the journey to be easy, but snow, turbulent rivers, and hostile wildlife made every paw step a challenge. The lowest point came when Bright Stream died, snatched away by an eagle the cats were trying to hunt. Gray Wing, who was unable to save her, blamed himself for Bright Stream's death, and for the death of her and Clear Sky's unborn kits.

When they reached their new home, the mountain cats settled on the moor. Gray Wing preferred having the sky above his head to tree branches, and was dismayed when Clear Sky and some of the other mountain cats left the moor for the denser forest. He grew close to a loner named Storm but she became Clear Sky's mate instead, then left the forest when she was expecting his kits. Gray Wing went to look for her, finding her just as the abandoned Twoleg den where she had given birth was being knocked down. Gray Wing risked his life to rescue one of the three kits, but was unable to save the rest of the litter or Storm. Gray Wing named the surviving kit Thunder and took him back to the moor to raise him when Clear Sky refused to have anything to do with his son.

Gray Wing was able to help both the moor cats and Clear Sky's group escape a devastating forest fire, but was permanently weakened by inhaling the smoke of that fire. After Tall

Shadow stepped back from leading the cats on the moor to care for her injured brother, Moon Shadow, Gray Wing emerged as leader in her place. His heart ached when Thunder, now almost grown, decided to leave the moor and live with Clear Sky, but he found love with his old friend Turtle Tail and helped to raise her kits as if he were their father. Although Gray Wing eventually stepped away from leadership and never became a true Clan leader, his clear-sighted compassion and his gift for planning battles meant that future generations of cats would know him as Graywing the Wise.

CLEAR SKY

CLEAR SKY

CLEAR SKY WAS ENTHUSIASTIC about the idea of leaving the mountains—unlike his littermate Gray Wing. He was in love with Bright Stream, who was expecting his kits, and persuaded her to join the group on their quest to find a new home. When Bright Stream was carried off by an eagle early in their journey, Clear Sky fell into a deep depression, blaming himself for her death.

Clear Sky began to recover as the cats settled into their new home, and he took the lead in establishing a camp among the trees where his talents for leaping and hunting high in the branches served him well. Separated from many of the cats from the mountains who had chosen to make a home in a hollow on the moor, Clear Sky encouraged rogues to join him. Gradually he grew so obsessed with keeping his cats safe that he established boundaries and set cats to guard them. He and his guards attacked any cat who crossed his borders, and no other cat was permitted to hunt there—not even his old friends from the mountains or his littermate Gray Wing could visit him without trouble.

Clear Sky also insisted that all cats should be able to care for themselves and contribute to the group, so when Jagged Peak injured his leg by falling from a tree, Clear Sky drove him out. When he met the rogue she-cat, Storm, Clear Sky fell instantly in love with her. She decided to live with him, but later left because she couldn't bear his obsessions and the way he ordered her around.

Storm bore Clear Sky three kits, but only one survived the collapse of the Twoleg den where they lived. When Gray Wing took the surviving kit, Thunder, to his brother's forest camp, Clear Sky rejected him. Later Clear Sky regretted this and after a fire ripped through the forest, he reconciled with Thunder and encouraged the young cat to come live with him.

However, Clear Sky retained his fierceness toward intruders and even his own cats, qualities that led Thunder to leave.

After the Great Battle, Clear Sky realized that his fierceness in protecting his larger group rather than any individual cat had led to horrifying violence. While still proud and protective of the cats under his leadership, he became less fierce toward the other cats in the forest, and gentler with the weaker members of his own group. He became the first leader of SkyClan.

JAGGED PEAK

JAGGED PEAK

JAGGED PEAK WAS THE brother of Gray Wing and Clear Sky, from a younger litter. As a kit he was bright and brave, impatient to get out of the cave and begin learning skills of hunting and mountain survival. When the cats cast votes whether to stay in the mountains or leave, Jagged Peak voted to leave and was frustrated when his mother, Quiet Rain, said that he was too young to go. Refusing to be left behind, Jagged Peak crept out of the cave and went after the departing cats.

He tracked the group for a good distance before he was attacked by an eagle and had to be rescued by Gray Wing, who had followed him. But his spirit stayed strong after the danger, and the two cats journeyed on together until they caught up with the group.

Jagged Peak especially admired his brother Clear Sky and went with him to the forest when the cats split into two groups. He enjoyed learning to hunt in trees but was badly injured when he fell from a high branch. As soon as it became clear that his injured leg wouldn't heal properly, Clear Sky banished him, and he returned to the moorland cats. Here he grew embittered because he felt he was useless. But Jagged Peak discovered an affinity for young kits and was able to become a valued member of the group on the moor by the care he gave them. While his limp never fully disappeared, he gradually became stronger and was eventually able to raise his own family in WindClan.

THUNDER

THUNDER

THE SON OF STORM and Clear Sky, Thunder was born in the Twolegplace and rescued from a collapsing Twoleg den by his father's brother, Gray Wing, who took him to Clear Sky's camp in the forest. He was bewildered by Clear Sky's rejection of him, and anxious about what would happen to him, until Gray Wing brought him to the moor and persuaded the moorland cats to take him in.

Though Thunder was raised on the moor, his instincts were to hunt among trees, using cover to creep up on his prey, and he found it hard to hunt on the open land, where there was nowhere to hide. But he worked hard to perfect his skills, wanting to make Gray Wing proud.

Thunder's first chance to shine came during the forest fire. He was the first cat to leap over the flames when River Ripple showed the cats the way to safety, and joined Jackdaw's Cry in returning through the flames to rescue Moon Shadow.

After the fire, Clear Sky and the other forest cats temporarily took shelter with the cats on the moor, and Clear Sky was impressed with the promise of his strong young son. Thunder was proud to be praised by his father, and went with Clear Sky when the forest cats returned to their camp. But Clear Sky's aggressiveness alienated Thunder's compassionate nature, and when Clear Sky drove another cat, Frost, out to die, Thunder went with him, taking him to the moorland camp.

While he struggled to find the place where he truly belonged, Thunder was always strong and determined. He fought bravely in the Great Battle and won the respect of the cats around him. In the end he became the first leader of ThunderClan.

STORM AND
TURTLE TAIL

STORM AND TURTLE TAIL

STORM WAS A LONER, a beautiful she-cat with silver fur and green eyes. She had no permanent home, but moved easily between the forest and the Twolegplace. The first mountain cat she knew was Gray Wing. Though she teased him, she clearly liked him and was happy to spend time with him in the forest, but when she met Clear Sky, the two cats instantly fell in love.

Storm went to live with Clear Sky, but gradually became disillusioned. She could not approve of Clear Sky's obsession with guarding his territory and controlling his cats' lives, or his violent clashes with trespassers. She felt guilty because she didn't speak up when Clear Sky drove Jagged Peak out of the forest. As an independent, spirited cat, she also became impatient with Clear Sky when he tried to pamper her while she was carrying his kits.

Finally Storm couldn't stand Clear Sky's ways any longer and grew tired of making excuses for him. She left the forest and made a nest in an abandoned Twoleg den, where she had her kits. She and two of her kits died when Twolegs demolished the den; Gray Wing rescued the third kit, Thunder. In his grief, Clear Sky was unable to forgive himself for driving Storm away and would not accept Thunder into his group.

Despite her death, the memory of Storm continued to affect Gray Wing and Clear Sky for many moons, and Thunder would always yearn for the mother he could barely remember

Turtle Tail had tortoiseshell fur and green eyes; her name came from her stumpy tail. She was part of the group of cats who came from the mountains, and remained on the moor when the group split into two. She befriended a kittypet named Bumble and spent a lot of time with her, even visiting her home in the Twolegplace.

Always cheerful and brave, Turtle Tail's natural optimism was tried when she fell in love with Gray Wing, who at first only regarded her as a friend. She was hurt when Gray Wing became interested in Storm and, feeling rejected, she went to live with Bumble and her Twolegs.

When the Twolegs brought another kittypet named Tom into their home, Turtle Tail thought she might be able to make a life with him and became pregnant with his kits. But when Bumble admitted that the Twolegs would take her kits away from her, she left the Twolegs and returned to the moor.

At first Turtle Tail was unsure whether her former denmates would welcome her back, and some of them were hostile to admitting a cat who had chosen to be a kittypet. But Gray Wing spoke up for her; while she was away he had missed her dreadfully, and now he realized how much she meant to him. Turtle Tail finally had the life she'd dreamed of when she and Gray Wing became mates, and Gray Wing became father to her kits, Pebble Heart, Owl Eyes, and Sparrow Fur.

TALL SHADOW

TALL SHADOW

TALL SHADOW WAS A thick-furred, black she-cat with green eyes. She left the mountains with Clear Sky and the others and became the leader of the group after the death of Shaded Moss.

She was always a watchful and thoughtful cat, tending to be suspicious of strangers. She was reluctant to allow other cats to join the group and at first sent Gorse and Wind away, even though the rest of the group would have welcomed them in. This caused a quarrel among her cats; some of them even called for her to step down as leader and for Gray Wing to take her place, though Gray Wing himself had no wish to do this. Her insistence on watching the camp also angered some cats, who felt that she should be taking a more active leadership role.

However when her littermate, Moon Shadow, was badly injured in the forest fire and later died, Tall Shadow found her anxiety and grief was too much to bear. She willingly gave up the leadership to Gray Wing, although later she resumed her authority and for a time the two cats acted as joint leaders.

Eventually Tall Shadow became the first leader of ShadowClan and led her cats into new territory across the Thunderpath.

dappled pelt and
cloud spots

Dappled Pelt and Cloud Spots

DAPPLED PELT WAS A tortoiseshell she-cat with a compassionate nature and an instinctive talent for healing. She was interested in herbs and had an excellent memory for which ones were the best to treat her denmates' injuries and illnesses. She came with the cats from the mountains and settled on the moor with Tall Shadow's group.

When Jagged Peak was injured by falling from the tree, Dappled Pelt went to the forest and lived for some moons with Clear Sky's cats while she took care of him. But her loyalty to the moorland group never wavered and she was glad to return home.

On first leaving the mountains, Dappled Pelt discovered a natural affinity for the water, learning to fish minnows from the river with her paws. While exploring the moor, she became good friends with the helpful and friendly River Ripple and was delighted to find a lush growth of herbs around the river. After the Great Battle, she soon found her true home by the riverside, joining River Ripple's group of cats and eventually becoming the first medicine cat of RiverClan.

A long-furred, black tom, with white ears and chest and two white paws, Cloud Spots was a mountain cat who settled on the moor. He was interested in healing, particularly in figuring out why certain herbs worked on certain illnesses, and in researching more curative plants. He

and Dappled Pelt were close friends and worked well together, her warmer nature complementing his focus on the effects of different herbs. He was not a strong fighter and in fact did not participate in the Great Battle, instead staying in the moor cats' hollow, preparing to treat injuries from the battle.

Cloud Spots was a shy and reserved cat, which made it harder for him to show his compassion toward his patients, and he tended to be brusque with them. He was especially impatient when dealing with sickly kits, often explaining in great detail the effects of a particular herb rather than sympathizing with a kit's aches and pains. He did, however, form a close bond with young Pebble Heart, who would one day become ShadowClan's first medicine cat, and taught the kit all he knew about herbs and the treatment of illnesses and injuries.

Despite the time he spent on the moor, Cloud Spots was happier in the dense undergrowth of the forest. When Thunder left the moor for the forest after the Great Battle, Cloud Spots went with him and settled there. He would become the first medicine cat of ThunderClan.

WIND RUNNER

WIND RUNNER

WIND RUNNER WAS ORIGINALLY a loner named Wind, who lived on the moor before the arrival of the mountain cats. With her mate, Gorse, she was hostile when they first arrived, accusing them of stealing prey. But gradually both cats grew to appreciate the advantages of living with a group.

A thin and wiry cat, Wind was able to race across the moors speedily and was a good hunter. She would even follow rabbits down into their burrows, as brave and quick below-ground as she was out in the open. She showed Gray Wing and the other moor cats this way of hunting, though Gray Wing felt trapped in the narrow, dark spaces. When Jagged Peak was trapped in a tunnel collapse, Wind and Gorse were able to dig him out and clear his nose and mouth of dirt so he could breathe again, saving the young cat's life.

Before long, Wind and Gorse became regular visitors to the camp on the moor. For Wind, the turning point from loner to group member came when she realized she was expecting Gorse's kits, and she asked that she and Gorse officially become part of the camp, eager for her kits to have the protection of this larger group. They willingly took longer names to be like the rest of the mountain cats, and Wind became Wind Runner.

Wind Runner was strong and intelligent, but some cats were wary of her because she tended to be pushy, making decisions that should have been made by the leader. While most of the mountain cats wanted to bring the two valuable cats into their group, they felt that Wind Runner was likely to take over.

After the Great Battle, Wind Runner naturally stayed on the moor, although she and Gorse Fur separated themselves and their kits from most of the mountain cats for a while, leaving the hollow. Eventually the tough and determined she-cat became the leader of WindClan.

GORSE FUR

GORSE FUR

QUIETER AND LESS EAGER to lead than Wind, Gorse, whom the moor cats renamed Gorse Fur, was nonetheless smart and observant, able to pick out prey at long distances from across the moor. Deeply loyal to his mate, Gorse Fur was willing to follow where she led, whether it was joining Tall Shadow and Gray Wing's cats on the moors or starting their own Clan after the Great Battle.

Despite this choice to follow Wind Runner, the thin, gray tabby cat had a mind of his own. He was always patient with other cats, often taking a whole day to teach restless kits the basics of hunting on the moor, and this patience and intelligence served him well, first as Wind Runner's deputy and, after her death, as the second leader of WindClan.

RIVER RIPPLE

RIVER RIPPLE

RIVER RIPPLE WAS AN elegant, silver-furred cat. He was very good-natured and most at home in and around the water. When the mountain cats arrived, he was a loner living beside the river at the edge of the forest. Though he was friendly toward the mountain cats when he encountered them, he was proudly independent and showed no interest in joining them. During the forest fire, it was River Ripple who showed the moorland cats how to escape the flames—and for that, they were forever grateful.

Long before the mountain cats came to the forest, River Ripple had grown up as one of another group of cats, far away. While he treasured his independence after coming to the forest, he accepted the role given to him by the spirits of former cats after the Great Battle and became an inspiring leader, the founder of RiverClan.

River Ripple was always willing to give other cats the benefit of his wisdom and experience, and so it is not surprising that he was the cat to first propose the system of formally apprenticing each young cat to an older warrior. This openness to sharing his knowledge with others is perhaps River Ripple's greatest legacy to the cats of the Clans.

← Worlds GREATEST Leader!

MOTH FLIGHT

Moth Flight

MOTH FLIGHT, A SOFT-FURRED, white she-cat with green eyes, was one of the first cats to be born to the group of cats living on the moor, the daughter of Wind Runner and Gorse Fur. She had a dreamy, restless, and curious nature, which at first made her seem unwarriorlike despite her swift feet and true heart. Gentle and playful, she was likely to be distracted from a hunt or battle by the discovery of a feather drifting across the grass or a bunch of berries growing on a bush. At one point, her distractibility almost led to Gorse Fur's death, when he had to shove her out of the path of a monster and was almost killed himself. In a rage, Windstar exiled her own daughter from WindClan.

But it was these qualities of imagination and curiosity that were to decide Moth Flight's destiny and lead her to the Moonstone. After her exile, Moth Flight followed the signs only she could see—a blowing feather, a flying bird—to a cave in the mountains beyond the Clans' territories. There, she found the Moonstone, and the spirits told her to take the knowledge of this sacred place back to the Clans. They told her to return to WindClan, that she would become the first medicine cat, and gave her visions of who the other first medicine cats, one for each Clan, would be. They explained that she and the other medicine cats would be not just cats with the knowledge of healing herbs, but responsible for seeing visions, interpreting signs, and guiding their leaders to make the best choices for their Clans.

Moth Flight, once an outcast, would always be remembered and admired by all the Clans as the first true medicine cat.

ANIMALS OUTSIDE THE CLANS

Introduction: Rock Speaks

EVER SINCE CATS FIRST decided to live together—in Tribes, Clans, whatever they chose to call themselves—there have been others that preferred to live alone. The Clans may believe that there is no way to survive except by the warrior code but, nevertheless, they have to acknowledge the tenacity of the Tribe of Rushing Water, the cheerful contentment of certain kittypets and rogues who have crossed their paths, even the ruthless battle-hunger of Scourge's BloodClan.

For the Clan cats, the warrior code has served them well, providing them with food and shelter and well-defended territories, as well as neighbors to turn to in times of great need. But the forest is not littered with the bodies of loners and rogues who have starved to death or been killed like prey, and kittypets do not swarm from Twoleg nests like bees to join their groups. There are other ways to live—ways that might suit some cats even better than being a warrior. And every so often, it is cats from outside the code that have shaped the destiny of a Clan.

RAVENPAW AND
BARLEY

RAVENPAW AND BARLEY

RAVENPAW'S FATE WAS SEALED the moment Bluestar appointed Tigerclaw to be his mentor. Ravenpaw was never going to be a ferocious warrior, leaping into battle at the head of a patrol. He preferred to seek peace through compromise and agreement. Tigerclaw saw this natural reserve as cowardice and pushed his apprentice to the point of hysteria. When Ravenpaw had the misfortune to witness Tigerclaw killing Redtail, then lying about it to their Clanmates, he put himself in more danger than he could have imagined.

Firepaw saved Ravenpaw from Tigerclaw's vengeance by taking him far from his forest home to the farm that the warriors passed on their way to the Moonstone. Here, Ravenpaw found the peace and freedom from borders that his heart had longed for. And most important, he found the dearest friend he would ever have: Barley, the plump black-and-white mouser who lived in a cozy barn with a feast of mice at his claw-tips.

Barley was no stranger to the horrors of bloodshed, though. He had been born in Twolegplace among the cats of BloodClan. When he insisted on staying with his littermate Violet, against Scourge's orders, he was forced to watch his sister being attacked by Scourge's closest supporters—none other than Scourge and Violet's remaining littermates. Violet barely survived and became a kittypet soon after. Barley escaped to the farm and lived in solitude until the happy arrival of Ravenpaw.

Neither of them forgot Ravenpaw's Clan origins, and they helped the cats from the forest many times over, joining the battle against BloodClan with relish and then allowing all four Clans to hunt and rest at their farm before they embarked on the Great Journey. Ravenpaw was much missed by his ThunderClan friends, but not a single one of them would have forced him to return to the place where he had known such abject misery because of Tigerclaw.

SMUDGE and
PRINCESS

SMUDGE AND PRINCESS

SMUDGE WAS THE WELL-FED, idle, black-and-white kittypet who first sensed Rusty's obsession with the wild cats in the woods. While Smudge was in no hurry to meet dangerous creatures that feasted on bones and lived by some obscure code that kept them in the cold, wet trees, he was a loyal and courageous friend to Rusty, who would become Firestar. When Smudge started dreaming of strange, far-off cats that seemed in dire need of help, he left the safety of his backyard and ventured into the forest to find Firestar. Who knows why StarClan would have sent dreams of SkyClan to a pampered kittypet? Perhaps the warrior ancestors have learned to be less judgmental of cats with a different lifestyle than the living Clans.

Princess was the pretty, fluffy littermate of Rusty's who went to live with different house-folk when they were still tiny kits. She had no idea what had happened to her brother until a chance encounter at the edge of ThunderClan territory. Although Princess had no wish to live by the rules of the wild herself, she was proud enough of her brother to give him her firstborn kit, Cloudkit, wishing for him the same noble life that Fireheart spoke of. The wisdom of her decision was questionable at times, especially in the beginning when Cloudpaw had difficulty settling into this tougher life, but it was a clear sign of Princess's trusting and hopeful nature. Firestar often thought of his sister, even when he had taken his Clan far from the forest to their new home beside the lake. And Princess still thinks of him, knowing he and her precious son have traveled far away, but with no means of finding out if they are still alive.

SCOURGE and BONE

SCOURGE AND BONE

[handwritten annotations: "No!" with arrow, "Hell No!" with arrow]

SCOURGE WAS BORN ON the edge of Twolegplace, the kittypet son of Quince and Jake, who went on to father Firestar and Princess with another kittypet, Nutmeg. Initially named Tiny, Scourge was a puny, protesting kit who was treated with dismissive scorn by his littermates, Socks and Ruby. Determined to prove that he was their equal, Scourge began exploring the woods that lay beyond the backyard fence. An encounter with a ThunderClan patrol led to his first fight, with the powerful apprentice Tigerpaw. Scourge was soundly defeated—and he never forgot the injustice of the uneven battle. He decided not to return home, but instead to live wild in Twolegplace, finding his own food and shelter.

Scourge tried to rip off his kittypet collar using an ancient dog's lost tooth, but the tooth got stuck in the fabric without loosening the collar one bit. If other stray cats chose to interpret this as a trophy from a fight with a dog that Scourge had killed, he had no intention of stopping them. His reputation grew among the Twolegplace cats, and Scourge felt the first seductive stirrings of power. He sought out the strongest, cruelest cats to support him and used them to punish weaker cats that disobeyed the rules he introduced. He called his disparate rabble of followers BloodClan, not that he had any interest in a code of honor like that of the forest Clans.

When a former BloodClan cat came to him with the leader of ShadowClan, asking for an alliance against the other Clans, Scourge recognized Tigerstar at once. He agreed to help, with no intention of falling in with Tigerstar's plans. When Scourge led BloodClan into the forest, he declared his real aim: to take over the whole forest as extra territory for his Twolegplace cats. Tigerstar protested, so Scourge killed him, ripping all nine lives from him with a single blow.

But the Clan cats were braver than he

anticipated and, in a ferocious battle, Scourge met his match in his half brother, Firestar, leader of ThunderClan. Scourge struck the first deadly blow, but Firestar had been given nine lives by his warrior ancestors and recovered to strike back. Without belief in StarClan, Scourge had only one life to lose and he died at Firestar's paws, leaving his rogues to scatter back to Twolegplace in shame.

Bone was Scourge's closest ally—never viewed by Scourge as his equal, but valued for his brute strength and absolute courage in the fiercest battle. He walked ahead of Scourge into the forest, and for a moment the Clan cats assumed that this huge, ferocious tom was the one who led BloodClan. He died in the same battle as Scourge, killed by a swarm of apprentices after he took the ThunderClan deputy Whitestorm's life. No cat could have doubted Bone's loyalty to his cruel leader, and perhaps it is a tragedy that he never had the chance to live the life of a true Clan warrior.

SOL

SOL

SOL WAS A GINGER, black, and white loner with a deep desire to destroy the warrior Clans. This anger came from an incident in his early life. An encounter with SkyClan cats led him to join their Clan in the gorge, but though he tried to fit in with his new Clanmates, he was too selfish, too impulsive to be guided by the warrior code. Trying to help Leafstar only caused more trouble and, in a last desperate attempt to impress her, Sol took three kits and hid them far from the gorge so that he could play a triumphant role in finding them. But his plot was discovered and Sol was banished from the Clan, and warned by Leafstar that he could never be a true warrior. From that moment on, Sol was determined to hunt down every Clan cat he could find and prove to them that their code was worthless.

Sol's luck turned when he met Midnight, the badger with a deep connection to the Clans. He used her to glean information about the Clans and when he arrived by the lake, he was able to use that knowledge to appear mysterious and wise to the Clan cats.

He went first to ThunderClan, insisting he meant no harm and that he was only curious about the cats he had heard so much about. But he quickly began sowing seeds of discontent, telling Jaypaw and Leafpool that a terrible darkness was coming. This coincided with Jaypaw's own vision of blackness descending upon the forest. But as Sol had no connection to StarClan, Leafpool was disinclined to listen to him, and Firestar sent Sol away.

During a ferocious battle on ThunderClan territory that involved all four Clans pitched against one another, the sun vanished, plunging the forest into the darkness that Sol had prophesied. His prediction of the eclipse was a fortunate guess: He may have foretold a "coming darkness" and the loss of the sun, but this could have been interpreted as any kind of momentous change to affect the Clans. The fact that the sun actually disappeared played monumentally to his advantage, and set Sol on the path that almost led him to destroy the Clans forever.

Sol soon found an able audience with Blackstar, who was already in the depths of despair because of the troubles faced by his Clan in their new home. Sol encouraged Blackstar to give up the warrior code, to let his Clanmates hunt for themselves and take care of their own ailments. Under Sol's influence, Blackstar forbade his warriors from attending Gatherings, and his medicine cats from going to the Moonpool.

ShadowClan began to collapse from within, to the dismay of other Clans. It fell to Jaypaw's faked StarClan sign to restore Blackstar's faith and lead to Sol's banishment. But that wasn't the last the Clans heard of this cat. When the warrior Ashfur was killed in mysterious circumstances, many ThunderClan cats believed Sol was responsible. Brambleclaw led a patrol to track him down, and the ThunderClan cats eventually found Sol in the ruins of Purdy's Twoleg den. They escorted both cats back to the hollow, where Sol was taken prisoner and accused of Ashfur's murder. All this time, Sol remained calm, poised, unruffled, as if he knew more than the warriors would know in a dozen lifetimes. The other Clans were outraged to learn that Firestar had brought the troublesome cat back to the lake and insisted he be exiled once and for all.

Seasons later, Sol came back to ThunderClan. Many ThunderClan warriors viewed him with deep suspicion, but others believed he had chased off a fox that had been about to attack a pair of apprentices, and welcomed him. Sol took advantage of the young cats who had barely known him before and encouraged them to plan an attack on WindClan. At the same time, he secretly visited WindClan to stir up anger toward ThunderClan. Luckily Dovewing and Ivypool overheard his plot, and ThunderClan was ready for the attack. In the battle, Hollyleaf took on Sol and defeated him, threatening to kill him if he dared show his face in the forest again. Sol left, but behind him lay fretful, disunited Clans, vulnerable to the influences of the Dark Forest.

Sol came close to destroying the Clans by the lake, but the code held strong, and Sol remained as alone and bitter as he had always been.

ROCK

ROCK

ROCK WAS DISCOVERED BY Jaypaw in the tunnels beneath ThunderClan after they moved to their home beside the lake. Rock was an alarming sight, lurking in the darkness: hairless, hunched, with bulging, sightless blue eyes. No cat knew when he first entered the tunnels—if, indeed, he had ever lived in the open air. He was already a legend when a young cat of the Ancients, Fallen Leaves, entered the tunnels to begin his initiation as a sharpclaw. Rock kept count of the cats who survived the test and made it back out to the hillside, marking each success with a scratch on a piece of wood.

Rock watched Lionpaw and Heatherpaw play in the underground cavern, tolerating the disturbance because so much solitude could weigh heavy, even on him. When three WindClan kits got lost in the tunnels and Jaypaw and Hollypaw joined the others to search for them, Rock revealed himself to Jaypaw, recognizing in the blind medicine cat someone who would understand the messages he had to pass on. He helped Jaypaw find the kits and escape from the flooding caves, and he sent his scratched stick out with them, to remind Jaypaw of the history he had stumbled upon.

When Jaypaw traveled to the mountains to stay with the Tribe of Rushing Water, Rock walked in his dreams and took him to the Tribe of Endless Hunting, showing him that there were ancestors other than just StarClan. More than that, these cats were connected to the Clans, because they had come from the lake and then sent some of their kin to settle in the forest. Rock, together with the Tribe of Endless Hunting, had been waiting for Jaypaw to come for a long time, knowing that the future of the Clans lay in his paws.

Rock guided Jaypaw to walk among the Ancients as Jay's Wing, where he played a crucial role in sending the cats to find a new home in the mountains. There was nothing Rock could do to prevent the battle with the Dark Forest, but he could show Jaypaw just how important it was that the cats beside the lake survived, keeping alive the circle of sharpclaws, prey-hunters, cave-guards, and warriors that had rolled out since the very first sunrise over the lake.

But he also blamed the very existence of the Three for the threat that faced the cats by the lake. If Jayfeather, Lionblaze, and Dovewing had not come, they would not have fulfilled the prophecy that involved the Dark Forest rising. In his rage, Rock blamed the Clans too, for clinging to the memories of the cats who had done them wrong, preserving their existence in the Place of No Stars and giving them enough power to walk in the dreams of restless warriors.

Rock didn't take part in the Great Battle, but he watched from the tunnels, knowing that the prophecy had come true and the Three—with Firestar—had saved the cats that lived beside the lake in this age. There would be others, and others after them. And Rock would watch over them all, tireless, blind, and alone in his underground world.

fAllen leaves

ꜰALLEN LEAVES

ꜰALLEN LEAVES LIVED BESIDE the lake many, many seasons ago, before cats settled in the mountains or the forest, before there was any sense of a warrior code or the Clans. As a young cat, he was sent into the tunnels to find his own way out, the test that had to be passed in order to become a sharpclaw—the Ancients' equivalent of a warrior, though without the rigid structure of patrols and duties that came with the code of the Clans. Fallen Leaves never escaped the tunnels; the river flooded, trapping him forever, leaving his mother, Broken Shadow, to grieve endlessly. His spirit stayed in the tunnels, restlessly searching for daylight and fresh air, watching the rare cats who strayed down that far, wishing he could join their games.

Hollyleaf escaped into a collapsing tunnel when the truth came out that Leafpool and Crowfeather were her parents. She fled into the darkness and wandered lost and hungry, until Fallen Leaves found her and brought her a fish to eat and soaked moss to drink. He treated her injured leg with comfrey and showed her how to survive underground, fishing in the shadowy river and learning the fastest ways out—although Fallen Leaves was unable to follow her into the open.

For several joyous moons, Fallen Leaves was happier than he had ever been. But Hollyleaf grew restless, and Fallen Leaves knew that her heart lay with her Clanmates. He encouraged her to be true to herself, to go back and trust the love of her kin and friends to welcome her back to her home. His heart broke when she left, because it was the sharpest reminder yet that he could not share a life in daylight.

When Dark Forest warriors burst into the forest, Fallen Leaves finally broke free from the tunnels. Running alongside his mother, Broken Shadow, he leaped into battle and fought alongside Hollyleaf. He was there when she died, struck down by Hawkfrost. Fallen Leaves realized she would never be able to keep her promise and see him again, because she would walk a different path from him forever now. But the battle with the Dark Forest had finally set him free, and when peace settled on the lake, Fallen Leaves stayed with Broken Shadow and the rest of the Ancients, lost in the mist of long-forgotten memories, but free from the confines of the caves.

MIDNIGHT

MIONIGHT

MIDNIGHT WAS FIRST MENTIONED in the dreams of four cats, one from each Clan, who were told to "meet at the new moon and listen to what midnight tells you." Baffled, Brambleclaw, Crowpaw, Tawnypelt, and Feathertail set out on the quest, accompanied by Squirrelpaw and Stormfur. Eventually their journey led them to steep sandy cliffs beside the sun-drown-place, where they discovered that Midnight was not a moment of darkness but a living, breathing creature: a badger, enemy to all the cats. But this badger was different. She could speak their language, more or less, and she was only hostile until she realized where they had come from. She told them that all four Clans had to leave the forest before the Twolegs destroyed it. To find a new home, they must stand on Highrocks and follow "a dying warrior," which turned out to be a falling star that led them to the lake.

Midnight appeared again when badgers attacked the ThunderClan camp in revenge for one that had been driven out when the cats first settled in the hollow. Midnight fought on the side of the warriors and helped defeat the badger hordes. Later, after Sol had come to the lake and done his best to cause trouble, Jayfeather met Midnight in his dreams and asked why she had told this loner so much about the Clans. Midnight replied that the Clans were about to face a challenge far greater than a curious stranger; she already knew about the threat rising from the Dark Forest, and had sent Sol to test the warriors' faith in their ancestors. If they could resist Sol's self-serving, destructive philosophies, they stood a chance of defeating the vengeful cats coming back from the dead.

She returned to the lake to help in the battle against the Dark Forest, fighting alongside the Clans to drive out their greatest enemies of all. Midnight was no ordinary badger: With Rock, she had watched the very first sunrise over the lake and had seen reflected in the fiery surface the futures of Clans, Tribes, Ancient cats, and more. Together, Midnight and Rock watched over the cats by the lake and prepared for the day that could have been the sunset of the ways of the Clans, but instead heralded a new dawn.

ERIN HUNTER

is inspired by a love of cats and a fascination with the ferocity of the natural world. As well as having great respect for nature in all its forms, Erin enjoys creating rich mythical explanations for animal behavior. She is also the author of the bestselling Survivors and Seekers series.

READ ON FOR AN EXCERPT FROM

DAWN OF THE CLANS

WARRIORS

BOOK ONE:
THE SUN TRAIL

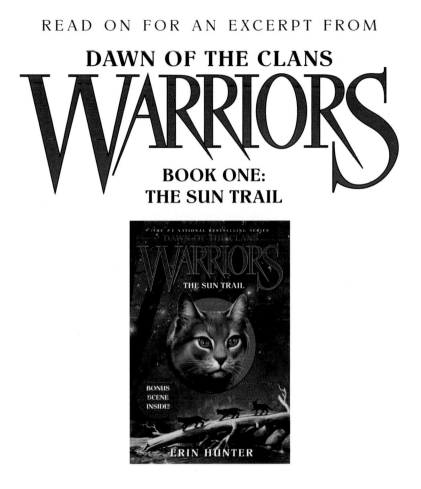

For many moons, a tribe of cats has lived peacefully near the top of a mountain. But prey is scarce and seasons are harsh—and their leader fears they will not survive. When a mysterious vision reveals a land filled with food and water, a group of brave young cats sets off in search of a better home. But the challenges they face threaten to divide them, and the young cats must find a way to live side by side in peace.

CHAPTER 1

GRAY WING TOILED UP THE SNOW-COVERED slope toward a ridge that bit into the sky like a row of snaggly teeth. He set each paw down carefully, to avoid breaking through the frozen surface and sinking into the powdery drifts underneath. Light flakes were falling, dappling his dark gray pelt. He was so cold that he couldn't feel his pads anymore, and his belly yowled with hunger.

I can't remember the last time I felt warm or full-fed.

In the last sunny season he had still been a kit, playing with his littermate, Clear Sky, around the edge of the pool outside the cave. Now that seemed like a lifetime ago. Gray Wing only had the vaguest memories of green leaves on the stubby mountain trees, and the sunshine bathing the rocks.

Pausing to taste the air for prey, he gazed across the snowbound mountains, peak after peak stretching away into the distance. The heavy gray sky overhead promised yet more snow to come.

But the air carried no scent of his quarry, and Gray Wing plodded on. Clear Sky appeared from behind an outcrop of rock, his pale gray fur barely visible against the snow. His jaws were empty, and as he spotted Gray Wing he shook his head.

"Not a sniff of prey anywhere!" he called. "Why don't we—"

A raucous cry from above cut off his words. A shadow flashed over Gray Wing. Looking up, he saw a hawk swoop low across the slope, its talons hooked and cruel.

As the hawk passed, Clear Sky leaped high into the air, his forepaws outstretched. His claws snagged the bird's feathers and he fell back, dragging it from the sky. It let out another harsh cry as it landed on the snow in a flurry of beating wings.

Gray Wing charged up the slope, his paws throwing up a fine spray of snow. Reaching his brother, he planted both forepaws on one thrashing wing. The hawk glared at him with hatred in its yellow eyes, and Gray Wing had to duck to avoid its slashing talons.

Clear Sky thrust his head forward and sank his teeth into the hawk's neck. It jerked once and went limp, its gaze growing instantly dull as blood seeped from its wound and stained the snow.

Panting, Gray Wing looked at his brother. "That was a great catch!" he exclaimed, warm triumph flooding through him.

Clear Sky shook his head. "But look how scrawny it is. There's nothing in these mountains fit to eat, and won't be until the snow clears."

He crouched beside his prey, ready to take the first bite. Gray Wing settled next to him, his jaws flooding as he thought of sinking his teeth into the hawk.

But then he remembered the starving cats back in the cave, squabbling over scraps. "We should take this prey back to the others," he meowed. "They need it to give them strength for their hunting."

"We need strength too," Clear Sky mumbled, tearing away a mouthful of the hawk's flesh.

"We'll be fine." Gray Wing gave him a prod in the side. "We're the best hunters in the Tribe. Nothing escapes us when we hunt together. We can catch something else easier than the others can."

Clear Sky rolled his eyes as he swallowed the prey. "Why must you always be so unselfish?" he grumbled. "Okay, let's go."

Together the two cats dragged the hawk down the slope and over the boulders at the bottom of a narrow gully until they reached the pool where the waterfall roared. Though it wasn't heavy, the bird was awkward to manage. Its flopping wings and claws caught on every hidden rock and buried thornbush.

"We wouldn't have to do this if you'd let us eat it," Clear Sky muttered as he struggled to maneuver the hawk along the path that led behind the waterfall. "I hope the others appreciate this."

Clear Sky grumbles, Gray Wing thought, *but he knows this is the right thing to do.*

Yowls of surprise greeted the brothers when they returned to the cave. Several cats ran to meet them, gathering around to gaze at the prey.

"It's *huge!*" Turtle Tail exclaimed, her green eyes shining as she bounded up to Gray Wing. "I can't believe you brought it back for us."

Gray Wing dipped his head, feeling slightly embarrassed at her enthusiasm. "It won't feed every cat," he mewed.

Shattered Ice, a gray-and-white tom, shouldered his way to the front of the crowd. "Which cats are going out to hunt?" he asked. "They should be the first ones to eat."

Murmurs came from among the assembled cats, broken by a shrill wail: "But I'm *hungry!* Why can't I have some? I could go out and hunt."

Gray Wing recognized the voice as being his younger brother, Jagged Peak's. Their mother, Quiet Rain, padded up and gently nudged her kit back toward the sleeping hollows. "You're too young to hunt," she murmured. "And if the older cats don't eat, there'll be no prey for any cat."

"Not fair!" Jagged Peak muttered as his mother guided him away.

Meanwhile the hunters, including Shattered Ice and Turtle Tail, lined up beside the body of the hawk. Each of them took one mouthful, then stepped back for the next cat to take their turn. By the time they had finished, and filed out along the path behind the waterfall, there was very little meat left.

Clear Sky, watching beside Gray Wing, let out an irritated snort. "I still wish *we* could have eaten it."

Privately Gray Wing agreed with him, but he knew there was no point in complaining. *There isn't enough food. Every cat is weak, hungry—just clinging on until the sun comes back.*

The pattering of paws sounded behind him; he glanced around to see Bright Stream trotting over to Clear Sky. "Is it true that you caught that huge hawk all by yourself?"

Clear Sky hesitated, basking in the pretty tabby she-cat's admiration. Gray Wing gave a meaningful purr.

"No," Clear Sky admitted. "Gray Wing helped."

Bright Stream gave Gray Wing a nod, but her gaze immediately returned to Clear Sky. Gray Wing took a couple of paces back and left them alone.

"They look good together." A voice spoke at his shoulder; Gray Wing turned to see the elder Silver Frost standing beside him. "There'll be kits come the warmest moon."

Gray Wing nodded. Any cat with half an eye could see how friendly his brother and Bright Stream had become as they stood with their heads together murmuring to each other.

"More than one litter, maybe," Silver Frost went on, giving Gray Wing a nudge. "That Turtle Tail is certainly a beautiful cat."

Hot embarrassment flooded through Gray Wing from ears to tail-tip. He had no idea what to say, and was grateful when he saw Stoneteller approaching them. She took a winding path among her cats, pausing to talk to each one. Though Stoneteller's paws were unsteady because of her great age, Gray Wing could see the depth of experience in her green gaze and the care she felt for every one of her Tribe.

"There's still a bit of the hawk left," Gray Wing heard her murmur to Snow Hare, who was stretched out in one of the sleeping hollows, washing her belly. "You should eat something."

Snow Hare paused in her tongue-strokes. "I'm leaving the food for the young ones," she replied. "They need their strength for hunting."

Stoneteller bent her head and touched the elder's ear with her nose. "You have earned your food many times over."

"Perhaps the mountains have fed us for long enough." It was Lion's Roar who had spoken from where he sat, a tail-length away.

Stoneteller gave him a swift glance, full of meaning.

What's that all about? Gray Wing asked himself.

His thoughts were interrupted by Quiet Rain, who came to sit beside him. "Have you eaten anything?" she asked.

All we ever talk about is food. Or the lack of it. Trying to curb his impatience, Gray Wing replied, "I'll have something before I go out again."

To his relief, his mother didn't insist. "You did very well to catch that hawk," she meowed.

"It wasn't only me," Gray Wing told her. "Clear Sky made this amazing leap to bring it down."

"You *both* did well," Quiet Rain purred. She turned to look at her young kits, who were scuffling together close by. "I hope that Jagged Peak and Fluttering Bird will be just as skillful when they're old enough to hunt."

At that moment, Jagged Peak swiped his sister's paws out from underneath her. Fluttering Bird let out a wail as she fell over, hitting her head on a rock. Instead of getting up again, she lay still, whimpering.

"You're such a silly kit!" Jagged Peak exclaimed.

As Quiet Rain padded over to give her daughter a comforting lick, Gray Wing noticed how small and fragile Fluttering Bird looked. Her head seemed too big for her body, and when she scrambled to her paws again her legs wobbled. Jagged Peak, on the other hand, was strong and well muscled, his gray tabby fur thick and healthy.

While Quiet Rain took care of his sister, Jagged Peak scampered to Gray Wing.

"Tell me about the hawk," he demanded. "How did you catch it? I bet I could catch one if I was allowed out of this stupid cave!"

Gray Wing purred excitedly. "You should have seen Clear Sky's leap—"

A loud yowl cut off Gray Wing's story. "Let all cats be silent! Stoneteller will speak!"

The cat who had made the announcement was Shaded Moss, a black-and-white tom who was one of the strongest and most respected cats of the Tribe. He stood on a boulder at the far end of the cavern, with Stoneteller beside him. The old cat looked even more fragile next to his powerful figure.

As he wriggled his way toward the front of the crowd gathered around the boulder, Gray Wing heard murmurs of curiosity from the others.

"Maybe Stoneteller is going to appoint Shaded Moss as her replacement," Silver Frost suggested.

"It's time she appointed some cat," Snow Hare agreed. "It's what we've all been expecting for moons."

Gray Wing found himself a place to sit next to Clear Sky and Bright Stream, and looked up at Stoneteller and Shaded Moss. Stoneteller rose to her paws and let her gaze travel over her Tribe until the murmuring died away into silence.

"I am grateful to all of you for working so hard to survive here," she began, her voice so faint that it could scarcely be heard above the sound of the waterfall. "I am proud to be your Healer, but I have to accept that there are things even I cannot put right. Lack of space and lack of food are beyond my control."

"It's not your fault!" Silver Frost called out. "Don't give up!"

Stoneteller dipped her head in acknowledgment of the elder's support. "Our home cannot support us all," she continued. "But there is another place for some of us, full of sunlight and warmth and prey for all seasons. I have seen it . . . in my dreams."

Utter silence greeted her announcement. Gray Wing couldn't make sense of what the Healer had just said. *Dreams? What's the point of that? I dreamed I killed a huge eagle and ate it all myself, but I was still hungry when I woke up!*

He noticed that Lion's Roar sat bolt upright as Stoneteller spoke, and was staring at her, his eyes wide with astonishment.

"I believe in my heart that the other place is waiting for those of you who are brave enough to make the journey," Stoneteller went on. "Shaded Moss will lead you there, with my blessing."

The old white cat glanced once more around her Tribe, her gaze full of sadness and pain. Then she slid down from the top of the boulder and vanished into the tunnel at the back of the cave, which led to her own den.

A flood of shocked speculation passed through the rest of the cats. After a couple of heartbeats, Shaded Moss stepped forward and raised his tail for silence.

"This has been my home all my life," he began when he could make himself heard. His voice was solemn. "I always expected to die here. But if Stoneteller believes that some of us must leave to find the place of her dream, then I will go, and do my best to keep you safe."

Dappled Pelt sprang to her paws, her golden eyes shining. "I'll go!"

"So will I!" Tall Shadow added, her sleek black figure tense with excitement.

"Are you flea-brained?" Twisted Branch, a scraggy brown tom, stared incredulously at the two she-cats. "Wandering off with no idea where you're heading?"

Gray Wing remained silent, but he couldn't help agreeing with Twisted Branch. The mountains were his home: He knew every rock, every bush, every trickling stream. *It would tear my heart in two if I had to leave just because Stoneteller had a dream.*

Turning to Clear Sky, he was amazed to see excitement gleaming in his brother's eyes. "You're not seriously considering this?" he asked.

"Why not?" Clear Sky demanded in return. "This could be the answer to all our problems. What's the point of struggling to feed every mouth if there's an alternative?" His whiskers quivered eagerly. "It will be an adventure!" He called out to Shaded Moss: "I'll go!" Glancing at Bright Stream, he added, "You'll come too, won't you?"

Bright Stream leaned closer to Clear Sky. "I don't know . . . would you really go without me?"

Before Clear Sky could reply, little Jagged Peak wormed his way forward between his two older brothers, followed by Fluttering Bird. "I want to go!" he announced loudly.

Fluttering Bird nodded enthusiastically. "Me too!" she squeaked.

Quiet Rain followed them, and drew both kits closer to her with a sweep of her tail. "Certainly not!" she meowed. "You two are staying right here."

"You could come with us," Jagged Peak suggested.

His mother shook her head. "This is my home," she said. "We've survived before. When the warm season returns, we'll have enough to eat."

Gray Wing dipped his head in agreement. *How can they forget what Quiet Rain told me when I was a kit? This place was promised to us by a cat who led us here from a faraway lake. How can we think of leaving?*

Shaded Moss's powerful voice rose up again over the clamor. "No cat needs to decide yet," he announced. "Give some thought to what you want to do. The half-moon is just past; I will leave at the next full-moon along with any—"

He broke off, his gaze fixed on the far end of the cave. Turning his head, Gray Wing saw the hunting party making their way inside. Their pelts were clotted with snow and their heads drooped.

Not one was carrying prey.

"We're sorry," Shattered Ice called out. "The snow is heavier than ever, and there wasn't a single—"

"We're leaving!" some cat yowled from the crowd around Shaded Moss.

The hunting party stood still for a moment, glancing at one another in confusion and dismay. Then they pelted down the length of the cavern to listen as their

Tribemates explained what Stoneteller had told them, and what Shaded Moss intended to do.

Turtle Tail made her way to where Gray Wing was sitting and plopped down beside him, beginning to clean the melting snow from her pelt. "Isn't this great?" she asked between licks. "A warm place, where there's plenty of prey, just waiting for us? Are you going, Gray Wing?"

"I am," Clear Sky responded, before Gray Wing could answer. "And so is Bright Stream." The young she-cat gave him an uncertain look, but Clear Sky didn't notice. "It'll be a hard journey, but I think it'll be worth it."

"It'll be *wonderful*!" Turtle Tail blinked happily. "Come on, Gray Wing! How about it?"

Gray Wing couldn't give her the answer she wanted. As he looked around the cave at the cats he had known all his life, he couldn't imagine abandoning them for a place that might only exist in Stoneteller's dreams.

THE TIME HAS COME
FOR DOGS TO RULE THE WILD

SURVIVORS

BOOK ONE:
THE EMPTY CITY

Lucky is a golden-haired mutt with a nose for survival. Other dogs have Packs, but Lucky has always stood on his own . . . until the Big Growl strikes. Suddenly the ground splits wide open. The longpaws disappear. And enemies threaten Lucky at every turn. For the first time in his life, Lucky needs to rely on other dogs to survive. But can he ever be a true Pack dog?

RETURN TO THE WILD

BOOK ONE:
ISLAND OF SHADOWS

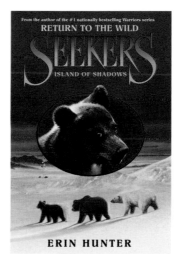

Toklo, Kallik, and Lusa survived the perilous mission that brought them together. Now, after their long, harrowing journey, the bears are eager to find the way home and share everything they've learned with the rest of their kinds. But the path that they travel is treacherous, and the strangers they meet could jeopardize everything the Seekers have fought for throughout their quest.

WARRIORS: THE NEW PROPHECY

Follow the next generation of heroic cats as they set off on a quest to save the Clans from destruction.

WARRIORS: POWER OF THREE

Firestar's grandchildren begin their training as warrior cats.
Prophecy foretells that they will hold more power than any cats before them.

WARRIORS: OMEN OF THE STARS

Which ThunderClan apprentice will complete the prophecy that foretells that three Clanmates hold the future of the Clans in their paws?

Visit www.warriorcats.com for the free Warriors app, games, Clan lore, and much more!

HARPER
An Imprint of HarperCollinsPublishers

WARRIORS STORIES

Download the separate ebook novellas or read them all together in the paperback bind-up!

DON'T MISS THE STAND-ALONE ADVENTURES

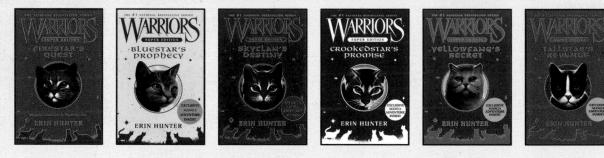

DELVE DEEPER INTO THE CLANS

Visit www.warriorcats.com for the free Warriors app, games, Clan lore, and much more!

HARPER
An Imprint of HarperCollinsPublishers

WARRIOR CATS COME TO LIFE IN MANGA!

Visit www.warriorcats.com for the free Warriors app, games, Clan lore, and much more!

HARPER
An Imprint of HarperCollinsPublishers

SEEKERS

Three young bears . . . one destiny. Discover the fate that awaits them on their adventure.

Seekers: Return to the Wild

The stakes are higher than ever as the bears search for a way home.

Available in Manga!

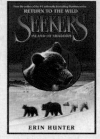    

www.seekerbears.com

SURVIVORS

The time has come for dogs to rule the wild.

www.survivorsdogs.com

HARPER
An Imprint of HarperCollinsPublishers